Karen D. McIntyre

Published by:
Lew & Karen McIntyre, Authors, LLC
11891 Knollcrest Ln
La Plata, MD 20646

Library of Congress Control Number 2018906745

Subjects: Fiction, Historical fiction, Depression-era, Appalachia, Women's issues, Abuse and recovery
ISBN-13: 978-1720347248
ISBN-10: 1720347247
Printed in USA

DEDICATION

Ruby began life as a character sketch. It was never intended to be a novel, but the character sketch became a short story, the short story became a novel, and here we are. It is a story that both wanted to and needed to be told. I am so very grateful to all the people who encouraged me along the way, especially my husband, Lew. He is my biggest cheering section, and my best sounding board/critic. Many thanks to my editor, Emily R. Antonen. I learned a lot from her, and she was adept at finding those places where I went astray. I couldn't have written Ruby's story without Lew and Emily. Thanks also to Dr. Shaheer Yousaf and cousins Kathy and Gracia – their knowledge and input was much appreciated.

Contents

ONE

GOING HOME

October 1932
Norfolk, Virginia

The bus was late. Rain clouds scudded across a leaden October sky as Ruby wrapped her arms around herself. Her thin sweater did little to counter the chill wind of the approaching storm. She nervously fingered the half dollar in her pocket, hoping it would last her until she got home. After buying her bus ticket, it was all the money she had left after five years of teaching.

I sure hope the bus gets here before the rain does, she thought, hunching her shoulders. *Finally*. The bus rounded the corner and stopped in front of her in a chuff of brakes and a swirl of exhaust.

Surrendering her ticket to the bus driver, Ruby took a seat a few rows behind him, staring out the window as rain began to streak the glass. The bus smelled of cigarettes and stale sweat, the faces of the handful of passengers reflecting a mix of the

1

numbness and despair she also felt. She hated that she'd lost her job, but at least there was the family farm to go back to until things got better. It was a ten-hour ride from Norfolk to Roanoke, so Ruby pulled a battered paperback from her satchel, preparing to read while there was still some light. The book slipped from her hand and landed in the aisle.

"Here, let me get that for you." The man sitting across the aisle from her picked up the paperback and held it out to her. "My name's Ray."

"Thank you, sir. I'm Ruby."

"Nice meetin' up with you, Miss Ruby." Ray extended his hand across the aisle for her to shake. "Looks like you've read that book a few times," he said with a smile. "One of your favorites?"

She laughed. "Never read it, actually. My landlady handed it to me when I was leavin' so I'd have somethin' to read on the bus."

For the next hour, as the bus rattled along, they talked about their favorite books. Ruby knew well enough to be cautious of strangers, but as they talked, she let her guard down. The man looked as down on his luck as she was, his tan overcoat worn, one pocket torn off, hair threaded with a bit of gray, and what looked like a two or three-day growth of beard.

He pulled a candy bar out of his one coat pocket, unwrapping it. As he went to take a bite, he noticed her watching him with something akin to longing on her face. "Do you want a bite of my Snickers bar?" he asked, offering it to her. "I don't mind sharing."

"Really?" she asked, her face brightening. "Thanks. I haven't had any candy in a long time, and my breakfast wore off a while back." She broke off a piece and reluctantly handed the candy bar back to Ray, the flavors of chocolate and peanuts exploding in her mouth.

"I know it's none of my business, but what puts you on this bus?" Ray asked, looking at her as he finished off the candy bar in two bites.

"I was teachin' in Norfolk. The state of Virginia decided to make ends meets by cutting money for the schools. Then Norfolk decided to close the kindergartens, and I lost my job. There's no work to be had in town, so I'm headin' back to my folks' farm for a bit. At least there I won't go hungry, and I can help out."

Ray shook his head. "That's awful! I'd heard they might do that. I got let go too, but the foreman promised to hire me back in six months. Hope he's not lyin'."

"What'll you do till then?"

"My brother says he's got somethin' to tide me over once I get to Roanoke. He's good at finding things, and I guess I'll help him." He looked at her, considering. "Where's your family's place? On past Roanoke, I'm guessin'."

"Yeah, about an hour up into the hills west of town. A long walk, but no help for it." Ruby glanced ruefully at her dress shoes. "Hope these hold up, but I'll make it one way or another."

"You mean your folks ain't meetin' you? How come?"

"I didn't rightly know which bus I'd be on, so I couldn't tell them when to meet me. They know I'm comin', just not exactly when."

"You know it'll be night when we get into town, don't you? Surely you can't be plannin' to walk an hour in the hills in the dark."

Ruby laughed. "Nope. Too many wild critters in those hills for that. I'll wait at the sheriff's station for first light and then set out. Sheriff won't mind."

"Maybe I can help you out some. My brother should be meetin' me with his old car. If he's got enough gas, I'll try to convince him to take you most of the way."

"That'd be mighty appreciated, but I wouldn't like to impose. Won't he think it odd you showin' up with me in tow?"

"Nah. He's used to me showin' up with new friends. If you don't mind, I think I'm gonna nap a bit now." Closing his eyes, Ray leaned his head against the bus window.

Ruby shifted on the hard bus seat, trying to get comfortable. *Maybe my luck is changing,* she thought. *It couldn't get much worse.* She'd been crushed when Norfolk closed the kindergartens because of the state funding cuts.

I tried to find another job, but there were none to be had. My students meant everything to me, that and being able to stand on my own two feet. I love my folks, and they'll be right glad to have me back, but after five years on my own in Norfolk, it's going to be hard to go back to living on a small farm.

She looked at her tired reflection in the bus window as the rain fell harder. It had been raining on her last day with her students too. It broke her heart when they all gathered around her for one last hug. As they left with their parents, little Bobby McAllister ran back to her, flinging his arms around her legs and hanging on tightly.

"No! You stay! I keep you," he cried out. Instead of his usual gap-toothed grin, Ruby saw tears trailing down his cheeks. She sank to the floor with him on her lap, assuring him she'd come back as soon as she could.

I wonder if he knew he was my favorite in the class. Such a bright, happy little boy. And the auburn hair and freckles – it was like looking into a mirror, except for the gap between his front teeth. He even laughed at my jokes. Ruby smiled, her mind full of bitter-sweet memories. She leaned back against the seat and was soon asleep.

Two

DRUGGED

October 1932
Roanoke, Virginia

"Roanoke, ladies and gents. Roanoke," the bus driver called out as the bus stopped with a sigh of brakes in front of some darkened buildings. Ruby jerked awake, grabbed her satchel, and got off the bus with a handful of passengers. She watched as the tail lights disappeared down the street. The few remaining passengers dispersed, and Ruby found herself alone on the sidewalk with Ray.

"Too bad the diner's closed for the night." Ray gestured to the building behind them. "I could sure use a cup o' joe."

Ruby looked around nervously. "Does your brother know when the bus was supposed to get in? Everything's so dark." Just then, the lights of a car parked down the block flashed on, and the car rolled smoothly to where they stood.

"Here's Joe now. He musta been dozin', waitin' for me." Ray reached for the door handle.

"Look, maybe I should just head over to the sheriff's station and wait there till morning like I planned. No need to trouble you and Joe." Ruby gestured down the street and took a step away from Ray.

He stepped in front of her, blocking her path. "Wait a second. I'm sure it'll be okay with Joe." He called to his brother, "Joe, you don't mind givin' my new friend Ruby a ride, do you? She's headed out to her folks' place. I kinda told her you'd help out."

Joe stepped out of the large four-door sedan and faced them across the car. "Sure. I'm always glad to help out a pretty young thing. Hop on in. Where you need to go, Miz Ruby?"

Ray and Ruby settled into the back seat of the car, and she gave Joe directions to her parents' farm. "Just follow Marshall's Creek Road up into the hills a few miles. You can drop me at the crossroads there. Mighty obliged, Joe."

"I don't suppose you've got a thermos of your good coffee, do you?" Ray asked his brother. "It'd be just the thing right now."

Silently, Joe passed a thermos over the back of the front seat, and Ray poured Ruby a generous amount. She settled back into the seat, drinking the warm chicory-flavored coffee and starting to relax. "Ray, I'm sorry – I'm hoggin' the coffee."

"Only one cup, honey." He smiled a bit sadly at her. "I'll have mine when you're finished."

She drained the cup and passed it back to him. "There. All done." She watched, puzzled, as Ray put the cup back on the thermos. "Didn't you want shum?" In horror, Ruby realized that her speech was slurring, and she was feeling very drowsy. "You … shlipped me a mm-Mickey!" she accused.

"Sorry, Dollface, but these days we all gotta do whatever it takes to survive. And you're worth a lotta dough, a looker like you." Ruby tried to lunge for the door handle, but Ray grabbed her and held on until she stopped struggling and passed out. "I really am kinda sorry, ya know," he whispered to her.

Three

RUINED

October 1932

Ruby awoke slowly, confused and disoriented. Eyes still closed, she took stock of her surroundings. She smelled pine trees and the musty scent of none-too-clean bedding. At that thought, she sat up quickly, clutching the sheet. She was naked, in a small bed, in a small poorly furnished bedroom. Where, she had no idea. The last thing she remembered was drinking coffee with Ray. Then – nothing until she woke up just now. Who had stripped her? What had they done to her? She had no idea. But she did know she needed to get out of there.

The sound of a door slamming somewhere in the house spurred her to action. Ruby jumped off the bed and began searching the room for her clothes, or anything to put on. Nothing in the drawers of the rickety dresser. Nothing in the tiny closet. She tried the door, only to find it locked. Turning her attention to the lone window, she soon realized it was blocked so it wouldn't open more than the scant half inch it already was.

At the sound of the door opening, Ruby spun to find Joe leering at her from the doorway. She tried to shield herself as best she could with her hands.

"Good. You're awake. Now we can get around to my favorite part." Joe closed the door behind him, and walked toward her as she backed away.

"Joe. Please. Let me go. I won't say a thing. Please, Joe," she begged. As he viciously backhanded her, she reeled back, her head snapping to the side. She fell against the bed, whimpering.

"Never, ever, use that name again. You need to learn. Men will be addressed as 'Sir'. Only that. No names. Do you understand me?" As he talked, he kicked off his shoes, pulled off his shirt, and dropped his trousers, stepping out of them.

"No, Joe! Please, no!" Ruby tried to scoot back across the bed, but he was on her in a flash, backhanding her again.

"What did you call me?" he yelled in her face.

"S … Sir. Sir, please, no!" she sobbed, twisting under him.

"Better." He gently stroked the side of her face marked with his handprint. "Hmmm … looks like you may end up with a shiner there. Oh well," he shrugged. "That won't interfere with what I plan to do to you." As Ruby struggled against him, thrashing and pushing at him, he laughed. "Keep that up, honey. I like it when they fight me. Won't make a difference anyhow, but still …." He pinned her down with his body, forced her legs apart, and roughly slammed into her. Ruby cried out in pain as he ground himself into her body. As he continued slamming into her, she lay there whimpering, tears sliding across her cheeks to dampen the lumpy pillow under her head. With a loud grunt, Joe collapsed on top of her. After a few minutes, when she thought he was asleep, she moved to slide out from under him. "Not so fast. We're not done yet," and he pulled her against him. He took her two more times, none too gently. Her body felt the pain, but her mind had gone numb. The violation, the shame she felt, was all more than her mind could handle.

Two hours later, as he stood dressing, he kicked the side of the bed. "You. What's my name?"

"J …" she paused, blinking groggily, hand going to her still reddened cheek. "Sir."

"Good. See you remember that," and he left, slamming the door.

Feeling broken, in more ways than one, Ruby rolled onto her side, clutching the sheet, curling up and making herself as small as possible. There were no coherent thoughts in her mind, just fragments and pain. She heard the door open and close. Looking over her shoulder, she saw Ray taking off his trousers.

"My turn!" He grinned at her. Ruby cried out as he ripped the sheet off her, rolled her over onto her stomach, and lifting her hips, took her from behind. "You'll find I'm not as rough as my brother. And I'd rather you didn't fight me. But either way, I'll be doin' this to you as often as I can." As he talked, Ray continued grinding into her, until, with a loud shout, he shook with his release. A short while later, he rolled off and stretched out next to her.

"Why?" she whispered. "Why did you do this to me? I thought we were friends."

"It's a business, Dollface. We find strays like you. We break 'em in and train 'em up. Then we sell them off for a goodly amount of dough."

"Who would want me now? I'm ruined. I've been raped and … and ruined." Ruby started to cry again.

"You'd be surprised. Probably a brothel, but we'll see." At her gasp, he rolled her over again.

"Now let's see to some more of your training, shall we?"

Four

BROKEN

Ruby sat on the side of the bed, shaking. There was not a bit of her body that didn't ache, especially between her legs. She was miserable, but her mind was beginning to clear. She looked up at Ray as he continued to dress. "Where are we?"

Ray chuckled. "We're miles from nowhere. Maybe a hundred miles or so from Roanoke, I figure. These here woods are full of bear, too, so don't go gettin' it in your head you can run off. You wouldn't make it far before we found you, or a bear got you. And the beatin' you'd get – well, it wouldn't be worth it." He shook his head.

Wrapping the sheet around herself, Ruby followed him out of the room to the top of the stairs. She grabbed his arm. "How could you do this to me? What kind of animal are you, Ray?"

"One who plans to survive the mess this country's in! And don't ever call me anything but Sir again." He grabbed her by the shoulders and shook her hard. When he released her, her feet tangled in the sheet. She stepped back to find nothing but air under her feet. With a scream, Ruby tumbled down the stairs, landing at the bottom in a broken heap. There was pain, and then blessed darkness.

Ruby became aware of voices. "She needs a doctor, Joe. That leg is broke bad."

"You know we can't get one out here. Can't risk it. You know that."

"So what do we do? We can't just leave her like this."

"We could, but we'd lose a bunch of money if we did. Let's set the leg as best we can, and hope for the best." Saying that, Joe straightened Ruby's leg, pulling hard until the bones ground and then meshed together. She screamed once, then blacked out from the pain.

Five

TOM AND LIDA SEARCH

November 1932
Roanoke, Virginia

It was three weeks since Lida and Tom Malcolm had gotten their daughter's letter, and they were getting anxious. In the letter, Ruby told them she'd lost her job and was heading home. But first she had to pack up her classroom and her room at the boardinghouse. There was also one last possible job to check on, before she would be ready to leave. If that lead didn't pan out, Ruby said she'd be home in about two weeks, taking a bus from Norfolk and then walking up from Roanoke. Ruby didn't give them an exact date when she'd be arriving. That was the last they'd heard from her.

"Ruby should have been here by now, Tom. Or at least sent a letter if her plans changed. This just ain't like her!" Lida wrung her hands.

"You're right. I'm thinkin' we should let Jasper Carter know so he can be keepin' an eye out for her," Tom answered.

"The sheriff?" Lida's voice rose. "You think somethin' happened to her that he needs to get involved?"

"Doubt it, but it can't hurt. You find a couple of pictures of Ruby, and we'll go to town and let him know. We can show Ruby's picture around at the diner where the buses stop. See if anybody's seen her."

"Train station, too – maybe she came that way. Give me a minute to find those pictures. I have some from last Christmas when she was home."

It was a quiet ride into town, as both Lida and Tom were lost in their own thoughts, worrying about their daughter. Before showing Ruby's picture around, they met with the sheriff and filled him in on the situation.

"Sheriff Carter, she wouldn't just go off willingly and disappear like this. She'd have written us if her plans changed. Can you help us?" Tom pleaded.

"Tom, I'm glad you came to see me. Of course, I can help you. Come into my office and sit a spell while I make a few calls." The sheriff quickly checked with the hospitals in the area to see if there had been any unidentified women brought in over the last few weeks, dead or alive. There were none.

Tom sagged back in his chair. "Thank God! That's a relief."

"And they'll let me know if somebody does show up, but I don't expect that," Jasper added.

"We brought in some pictures of Ruby. Here, you keep one." Lida handed a picture to the sheriff. "We thought we'd show these others around at the diner and the train station. Maybe somebody's seen her."

The sheriff nodded. "That's a good idea. I'll be doin' that too. Maybe I can find some of the people who got off the bus that night. Let me know if somebody does recognize her, and I promise to let you know what I find out." He paused. "And I'll borrow ol' Hiram's coonhound and see if there's any sign of your girl on the way up to your place."

For the next two hours, Tom and Lida showed Ruby's picture around, with no results. After a while, the 'No, ma'am's' and 'Sorry, sir's' just blended together. There was one time, at the train station, when a man paused and looked closely at the picture a second time. But then he just looked at them, shook his head, and hurried off.

It was a quiet ride back to the farm. Tom and Lida had to put their trust in the sheriff to do what he could to find Ruby, but that didn't mean they would worry any less.

Despite all their efforts to find their daughter, after three months there was still no sign of her. Tom and Lida once more found themselves sitting in the sheriff's office.

"Know you tried with that coonhound, but we figured we'd look too. We covered every inch of the route from town to the farm, lookin' to see if she'd come to harm along the way – walked it four times, in fact. No sign of her. Nothin'." Tom twisted his hat in his hands.

"And talkin' to the bus driver did no good," added Lida.

"That's right," Tom continued. "When we finally found the right driver, he wasn't much help. Said he recollected a girl who looked kinda like our Ruby gettin' on in Norfolk 'cause she just beat the rain. He half remembered her talkin' to some fella on the bus too. Said he didn't recollect her getting' off at any of the three small towns the bus stopped at before pullin' into Roanoke. By then, it was dark and late. He figured Ruby must have gotten off there 'cause she wasn't on the bus at the next stop, but he couldn't swear to it."

"Pastor Tyree has had the congregation out askin' after Ruby in town too. But nobody's seen her. She couldn't just disappear like that! Sheriff, what else can we do?" Lida was beginning to panic.

Jasper leaned on his desk, chin on his hands. "I've had the same results. Nothin'. The only good thing is the hospitals haven't gotten anybody in."

"Well, that's a blessin'," Tom nodded.

"Look … I know you don't want to hear this, but … until we know otherwise, I think we have to assume, after all this time, that maybe Ruby chose to disappear for a while."

"No way would our girl fret her Ma like that! No way!" Tom thumped his fist on the edge of Jasper's desk. "She'd let us know if she changed her plans."

Lida started to cry softly. "So you're sayin' there's nothin' more to be done to find my baby girl?"

"Miz Malcolm, … Lida, I won't stop lookin' for her, but there's not much more any of us can do. I'll put her on the Missing Persons Report that goes out to all the counties, and I'll keep askin' around. But now … we gotta just wait and pray she comes back." The sheriff stood and came around his desk, taking Lida's hand in his. "I promise to let you know if I hear anythin'."

Tom shook the sheriff's hand. "Jasper, we're not ever gonna believe Ruby means to be missin'. But you're right too – there's nothin' else we can do for now. Thanks for your time."

After the Malcolms left, the sheriff sat at his desk, lost in thought. He hated having to let them down, but with no evidence to the contrary, it did look like Ruby may have gone missing on her own. He pulled the Missing Persons Report from his desk drawer, and added her name to the growing number of people who had simply vanished in the past year or so. He could cross off Bob Stoddert from the list. Just yesterday, they'd found his body in the woods behind his cabin. Looked like he'd run afoul of another 'shiner. But the growing number of young women on the list troubled him. Three, plus Ruby, now made it four young women who had gone missing in the past year. There didn't seem to be a pattern to it, but it didn't feel right to him either.

Six

A NEW ROUTINE

April 1933

The day started out pretty normal. As Ruby was cleaning up after breakfast, Joe came into the kitchen. "Gonna be company for supper tonight. See you make up somethin' really special now."

Keeping her head down, eyes focused on her hands in the sink's soapy water, Ruby asked, "How many should I plan on, Sir?"

"Dunno. Maybe just Ray and me and our special guest. Or he might bring a friend or two. Just feed us good, and make sure the girls are ready for us." Joe stepped up behind Ruby, and hands on her belly, pulled her back against him. "You be ready too. He might just enjoy havin' his way with a cripple. Never know." His hands slid under her shirt, to squeeze her breasts painfully.

23

At the sound of a soft sob, he turned sharply, pulling away from Ruby. Across the kitchen, Mary whirled to run out.

"Stop!" Joe yelled, and Mary froze in place. "Come over here." She slowly walked over to Joe, head down, her whole body quivering. Mary had only been at the house for about a week. She was a tiny thing, and Ruby suspected she wasn't the sixteen she claimed to be. Dealing with her new reality was especially hard for Mary, and Ruby wasn't sure which was worse – her almost trance-like silences, or her nightmares when she woke up screaming. "You don't sound like you're lookin' forward to tonight. That true?" Joe taunted, poking his finger up under her chin, forcing Mary to look at him.

. "No Sir. I mean … yes, Sir. …I … Oh, I don't know …" Mary stammered out as tears welled up in her eyes.

"Huh. Sounds to me like you need me to remind you 'bout a few things. And practice up for tonight." Joe grabbed Mary's arm and dragged her out of the kitchen. Ruby heard her sobbing and calling out for help as Joe pulled her up the stairs. The sounds stopped with the slamming of a door.

Ruby grabbed the edge of the sink in front of her, her tears falling into the now cool dishwater with small plops. She feared for Mary, but she knew from experience that any interference would only make it worse for both of them. She dried her face and hands on a ragged kitchen towel, and set about planning a nice meal for tonight.

At least I can make something special for the girls, too. Maybe we have enough flour left for biscuits and a cake. I'll have to check on that. And maybe, just maybe, one of the men will be kind. And maybe, just maybe, I can ask him to get a message out. Miracles do happen, you know, Ruby thought to herself as she set to work.

When Joe came downstairs a couple of hours later, Ruby looked up from the garden peas she was shelling. "Shall I go tend to Mary, Sir?"

Joe glared at her. "No names! You know that." He advanced on her.

"Yes, Sir. Sorry. I forgot, Sir." Ruby cowered away from him, anticipating a blow. "I meant shall I go tend the girl?"

"Nah. She's okay. Let her sleep up there for the day. She's gonna be busy tonight." With a rough chuckle, he adjusted his suspenders and sauntered on out of the house.

With a sigh, Ruby watched him cross the yard to the barn. She knew he'd be out there for hours now, tinkering with his beloved car. Ruby made it a point to always know where the men were – it made it easier to avoid them whenever she could.

Ma and Pastor Tyree taught me that hating is wrong, and we should love those that do us harm. But I guess my heart just wasn't listening. I do so hate that man! With all my being. His brother isn't much better. I guess it's wrong to pray for somebody to die, but I surely do. Forgive me, Lord, but I do!

Sometimes I wonder if this is worse than being in a brothel. I can't prevent what happened to me from happening to the girls Ray and Joe bring here. I can't do anything but wait and listen to the girls crying and trying to fight off the men. And then afterwards, after they're hurt and broken, I tend to them and give them what comfort I can. Which isn't much. I hold them as they cry. Wipe their tears, and help them get cleaned up. To a girl, they all try to scrub off a layer or two of their skin in the tub. I could tell them that won't make a difference. It won't remove the sense of violation and shame they feel. It didn't for me. But I don't tell them that. Let them hope. Let them have that little bit of comfort.

There have been six more girls in the past year, three of them still here. And each time, when I held one of those girls as she sobbed, it felt as if a little bit of my soul shriveled up and fell away. I fear for what I will become in another year or so.

If my leg hadn't healed up wrong after I fell down the stairs and broke it, I wouldn't have ended up with this awful limp. Joe tried to sell me off to brothels a couple of times, but there were no takers. I guess nobody wanted a cripple, so they kept me here at the house. I'm their housekeeper, and they force themselves on me whenever they want. I think Joe resents that he couldn't make money off me, because he seems to especially like to hurt me, to force my legs apart and take me as hard as he can.

Limping across the kitchen to fetch another bowl for the shelled peas, Ruby glanced out the window and saw the 'hen house' across the yard from the big house. Ray and Joe had thrown together a building of sorts to serve as a bunk house for the girls. Ray thought it was funny to call it the 'hen house'. The building had simple bunk beds, a pot-bellied stove, a slop jar and a cracked sink with a pump. At least the girls didn't have to go outside when it was cold.

They thought putting us out there would make us feel isolated and alone, but they miscalculated there. She smiled ruefully and shook her head. *They moved us out of the big house so they didn't have to listen to the girls crying at night. Giving us our own space, this hen house, turned out to be a blessing for us. Away from their watchful eyes, we can lean on each other for strength. Here, another woman's hug can make the pain and fear just a little less. We dare not make it look any less stark, except for maybe a leaf or two or a pretty pebble. If they knew what this building means to us, they'd take that away too. So when they lock us in at night, we huddle on our beds and wait a spell. Once we're sure Ray and Joe aren't coming back, we gather around the old stove and whisper, talking softly about the days before we ended up in this hellhole. A while back, one of the gals was a natural-born storyteller, and she spun us some fine tales. Until she got sold on. Her name was Margaret. I've tried to remember her stories and tell them for her, but I know I don't do them justice.*

Sometimes it feels like my heart is black and full of so much hatred and pain and anger that it'll burst. Why did this have to happen to me?

As she finished shelling the peas, Ruby kept an ear tuned, listening for any sound from Mary. There was none.

Seven

THE SHERIFF

It was getting on toward suppertime when Joe emerged from the barn, wiping his hands on a greasy old rag. He strode through the front door, calling out to Ruby. "Supper 'bout ready? My friend should be here shortly. I'm just gonna go wash up a bit."

"Yes, Sir. It's all done and keepin' warm now. I'll set the table soon as I know how many …." She trailed off when she realized she was talking to his back as Joe bounded up the stairs to the second floor. "Yes, Sir. Yes, Sir. Three bags full, Sir," she muttered to herself.

"You bein' disrespectful, girl?" Ruby whirled to find Ray standing at the side door, several large squash from the garden in his arms. "I'd hate to think you were, now." While Ray wasn't as harsh as Joe, he was still a willing partner in his brother's activities.

"No, Sir. Just commentin' on the supper what's in the oven keepin' warm. See?" Ruby opened the oven door and pointed in. "Three bags full — three pans of food ready to go. Fried chicken, peas, and biscuits."

"Okay. Be careful tonight. Joe's in a rare mood. This guy who's comin' out ... well, it means a lot. Just be careful." Ray headed for the stairs, but turned back to look at her. "Be sure to get me a list of what supplies you need from town so I can get them tomorrow."

As she glared at the doorway through which he'd disappeared, Ruby realized that Ray was another one she'd like to pray dead. Not only was he quite happy to be a part of his brother's enterprise, but he kept trying to act like the nicer brother, like someone who cared about the girls. That deceit was just too much to stomach. At least Joe was openly evil, while Ray tried to hide it.

Just then Ruby heard a car pull up in the yard. She looked out the kitchen window to see a man getting out of a dusty old sedan.. Her breath caught in her throat as she took in the man's uniform. "My God - a sheriff!"

In a flash, Ruby was out of the house, limping as fast as she could down the steps and across the yard. "Sheriff! Thank God you're here! You gotta get me and the other gals out of here. Joe and Ray are keepin' us here and won't let us go and they are rapin' us and makin' us do all kinds of awful stuff and you just gotta get us out of here ...." Ruby realized she was babbling, but couldn't stop herself, her relief making her light-headed. When she came to a stop in front of the sheriff, he reached out and grasped her arms.

"That so, Miss?" He looked down at her for a second, and then his lips twisted into a smirk. At the sound of the front screen door closing, Ruby half turned to see Joe standing on the porch grinning at her. "I take it you didn't tell her I know all about what goes on out here," the sheriff called to Joe as two more men got out of the car.

"Nah. I thought we'd surprise her." Addressing Ruby he said, "'Nuff foolishness. You know there ain't no help for you. Get that table set quick now. And roust out the girls. Get on now!" Joe laughed and swatted her rump as Ruby limped past him into the house, shoulders slumped in defeat. "Sheriff, gentlemen," he addressed the men, "come on in and enjoy yourselves. That gal's not much to look at, but she sure can cook."

Back in the kitchen, Ruby clutched the edge of the sink, staring out the window, but seeing nothing. So much had changed since she stood there this morning, and so little had not. Still kept, still abused, still treated like dirt. *Just for a second there, I thought we were saved, that the sheriff would help us get away*

31

from here. But he's not like Sheriff Carter back home. Carter wouldn't stand for this, but this sheriff's part of the whole mess.

Slowly she turned and opened the oven to retrieve the food warming there. Setting the platters on the dining room table in front the men, Ruby then went out to the hen house to rouse the girls so they could try to eat something before the night's 'festivities'. One of the girls went upstairs to get Mary, and once they came down, all the girls sat around the kitchen table, numbly staring at the food on their plates. Waiting.

Eight

MARY

"Finally," Ruby mumbled to herself as she sank down at the kitchen table with a cup of weak coffee. Breakfast was done, everybody fed. The sheriff and his pals had left a bit ago. The girls were in the bathroom trying to scrub off last night, and she could finally take a few minutes of a breather before she had to clean up the house. Ruby grimaced as she shifted on the hard chair. Seems the sheriff did cotton to a cripple after all, and he was none too gentle. And he enjoyed taunting her about how she had greeted him when she first saw him. At least now she had an idea where they were. On the rim of his badge it said "Sheriff, Dalton Va.". Ruby figured that meant they were not too far from a town of that name, somewhere south and west of Roanoke probably, but still in Virginia.

Ruby hadn't seen Mary this morning yet. When she asked Joe, he said he was letting her sleep in this morning, and not to ask again. He didn't like her asking.

With a sigh, Ruby stood up gingerly, just as Joe came into the kitchen. "You – get to cleanin' this place up. Our fun got messy last night." As Ruby passed him, he gave a harsh laugh and smacked her behind. "By the way, it seems the sheriff was a mite taken with you – he said to tell you he'll be back again to see you."

Ruby shuddered as she crossed the hallway to gather up the dishes left on the table from the men's dinner last night. She winced at the burn mark from a cigar carelessly thrown down that now scarred the table's once fine wood surface. "Pigs!" she muttered, carrying a load of dishes to the kitchen sink. The mechanical action of washing the dishes gave her something to focus on, something she could control, and acted like a balm to her bruised heart.

It took her an hour to set the dining room to rights and finish up all the dishes. The girls had checked in to see if she needed help, but she sent them on to get some sleep. They'd had a rough time of it last night, more so than she had. Never had she been more grateful for the folk medicine she had learned from her mother. Before they crossed over to the 'hen house', Ruby made sure each of them drank a cup of her special tea. Made from a tincture of wild carrot seeds, if was their "morning-after" tonic.

Between the tea and the rubbers most of the men used, it was unlikely one of the girls would end up pregnant. The one time that happened – Ruby still remembered Joe beating the girl until she lost the child. Since then, Ruby made sure the girls drank their tea regularly. Still no sign of Mary.

Ruby trudged up the stairs to gather the bed sheets. They could soak a bit before she washed them. Meantime, she could straighten and air out the rooms. Starting with the first bedroom, Ruby pulled the bed linens as she went, piling them in the hallway. When she reached the small back bedroom, the first thing she noticed was the blood on the bed. It was not all that unusual for there to be a bit of blood on the sheets, but this was more than a bit. Staring at the bloody sheets, Ruby was filled with a sense of foreboding. "Mary?" she whispered. Could something have happened? Could this be why she hadn't seen the girl this morning?

A sound outside drew her to the window. She looked down into the yard to see Joe and Ray heading toward the woods. Ray carried a shovel over his shoulder. And Joe … Joe carried a blanket-wrapped bundle over his. As Ruby watched, a slender pale arm slipped out of the bundle to wave lifelessly as the men entered the woods.

"Oh, Sweet Jesus … that's Mary," and Ruby sank to the floor in front of the window and sobbed.

Ruby had no notion of how long she'd sat hunched over on the hard plank floor. It was the cramping in her bad leg that brought her back to reality. "What'm I gonna do?" she muttered to herself. "I failed Mary." She swallowed hard to keep from crying again. "They musn't know I've seen them, or I'll be next. What'm I gonna do?"

Her mind a mass of whirling fears and doubts, Ruby gathered the bloody sheets off the bed, and gathering the ones in the hall as she passed, she headed down for the laundry area on the back porch, As she scrubbed at the stains in the deep tub there, she tried to figure out what, if anything, she should do now. Instinctively, she knew that she had to look and act as though nothing was amiss. Acting normal would keep her alive.

Once the sheets had been scrubbed and were soaking in the wash tub, Ruby went back into the kitchen to start on the stew for that night's supper. She was chopping up the vegetables when Ray walked in. "You 'bout done upstairs?" he asked.

"Sheets are soakin' while I get this goin'. I'll finish washing them after I'm done," Ruby answered without looking up. She set down the knife carefully, realizing she was clenching it in her fist. *What does it say about me, that I want these men dead, but I can't make myself take a life?* she wondered.

"Good. By the way, Mary left with the sheriff and his pals. They're gonna take her down the mountain for us, so you don't need to be concerned about her nomore." Ray turned to go, but turned back and added, "And the other gals will be leaving next weekend. You make sure they're ready, you hear?"

Just like that? Ruby thought. *Just like that, you pretend nothing happened?* "Yes, Sir. I understand," she answered, almost gagging on the words.

Nine

A DANGEROUS DECISION

July 1933

That night, as Ruby lay restless in her narrow bunk in the hen house, she realized that, without really trying, she had come to a decision. *I've gotta try to get out of here. According to Joe, we're way out here in the hills. That makes my chances of making it out of here next to none – but I can't stay here anymore. Ray said there were bears and mountain lions out there, but Margaret, before she left, said that wasn't true. Hope she's right. After what happened to Mary – I can't wait around for that to happen to some other girl ... or to me. What's left of my soul can't take it.* Her decision made, Ruby finally drifted off to sleep.

Over the next few days, Ruby finalized her plans for escape. While she wanted to simply bolt, she knew that wasn't the way. Given her gimpy leg, any trek through the mountains would take her twice as long as anybody else. And that meant she'd need a few things – a stout walking stick, better shoes, some food to last a few days, and a heavier sweater or jacket. It might be the middle of summer, but the nights in the mountains still got pretty cold. Water she figured she could get from the streams she'd find.

When she and the girls were sent to pick a batch of the wild blackberries that grew around the edge of the woods behind the house, she found a downed branch that would do as a walking stick. She shoved the branch back as far as she could under the berry bushes, figuring the prickly plants would make a good hiding place until she was ready.

What to do about her worn out shoes stumped Ruby. Just when she'd decided her only course was to come up with more cardboard to replace their worn out soles, she remembered something that gave her hope. When Ray first brought Mary to the house, she'd had on a good pair of sturdy shoes. And Ruby remembered thinking how odd it was that such a tiny person had such large feet – like Ruby did. Now, if she could just find those shoes, she'd be set. They didn't turn up when Ruby searched the hen house, but she hadn't expected they would. So when the bed sheets had finished drying on the clothes line, Ruby searched the small back bedroom where Mary had last been. There, under the bed, Ruby found the shoes. "Thank you, Mary," she whispered. Wrapping them up in a bunch of cleaning rags, she smuggled the shoes out to the hen house, hiding them under her bunk. Later that night, she tried them on, overjoyed that they fit.

One of the bedrooms also yielded a torn thin blanket. Ruby cut a large square out of it, which when folded on the diagonal became a large shawl. It would do as a wrap against the cold, and maybe even double as a blanket. One more problem solved.

Pulling together the small stash of food Ruby figured she'd need proved surprisingly easy. Over the next week, she managed to set aside four stale biscuits, two slightly withered apples, and several pieces of Ray's venison jerky that he was so proud of. She secured her stash in a drawstring cloth bag that she hid among similar bags of beans, flour and sugar in the pantry. Ruby knew she was risking a beating if Ray or Joe found it, but she figured the chance was slim enough to risk it. Now all Ruby had to do was wait for the right time, for a chance to be free again.

That chance came the next Saturday. The morning dawned bright and clear, a welcome sight after last night's storm. Ruby stood with the two girls next to Joe's old car in the yard. The girls waited silently and hollow-eyed. Ruby hated feeling helpless, knowing there was nothing that she could do to stop the girls from being sold on to brothels or worse. She hated the defeated slope of their shoulders and the sad look in their eyes. She wrapped the girls in a big hug, and they stood that way, lending each other what support they could, until the creak of the screen door announced Joe and Ray's arrival.

Ruby pulled back quickly. "They're ready, Sir," she said softly, looking at her shoes.

"Better be," Joe replied gruffly looking the girls up and down. "In the car with you now – one up front, one in back," he added.

As Ray brushed past to get in the back seat, Ruby asked, "How long you plannin' to be gone, Sir?"

Ray stopped and looked at her oddly. "Why? You got plans or something?"

"No, Sir! I was just wonderin' 'cause I want to do some heavy cleanin' in the house and wanted it done 'fore you get back," she stammered out, hoping he would believe her.

"Huh!" Ray grunted. "The usual, two or three days."

"Should I expect company? I can make sure one of the rooms is ready if it'd be needed." In the past, the men had sometimes sent one of their friends to visit the place while they were gone. She guessed it was their way of making her feel watched, so that she stayed put.

"Probably not. Unless your friend the sheriff decides to come callin'." With that, Ray snickered as he got in the back seat of the car, slamming the door.

Ruby watched the sedan pull away with conflicting emotions. She still felt guilty that she couldn't help the girls, and she felt somewhat complicit in their downfall. In her head she knew better, but in her heart she still felt guilty. She also remembered something Ray had said to her what seemed like a lifetime ago – about everybody having to do whatever they could to survive. As the sedan disappeared down the track into the woods, Ruby began to feel elated. She finally had the place to herself. Now was the time to put her plan into action. A wide smile, the first in a long time, lit up her face as she turned to limp back into the house. *Tomorrow morning I leave here,* she vowed to herself. *Gotta be ready for first light. I'll gather my stash and set out then.*

Ten

INTO THE WOODS

Ruby was up with the sun the next day, eager to be on her way. She couldn't decide if she was more excited or scared. Growing up on her parents' farm in the foothills near Roanoke, she had spent a lot of time out in the woods and hills. Her bad leg would be a problem, but she figured the long hike would be doable. What scared her was the thought that she might not make it, that the men might track her down. She doubted if she'd survive the beating that would follow. *But I can't stay here any longer. I don't think I'd survive with my soul intact if I did. So buck up, gal, and get movin'.*

Wearing Mary's shoes, with her shawl wrapped around her thin shoulders, Ruby went to collect her stash of food from the pantry. As she grabbed the cloth bag from its hiding place, the eggs on the shelf below caught her eye. *Might as well go with a full stomach. I think there's still part of a rasher of bacon too. I'll boil up the rest of the eggs to take with me while I'm at it.*

43

But I ain't washin' up! Half an hour later, her hunger satisfied and the dirty dishes defiantly left in the sink, Ruby pulled her walking stick from under the berry bushes, and entered the woods in what she hoped was a northerly direction, the morning sun on her right. *Any direction will do as long as it's away from here. But this just feels right, like maybe I'm pointed to Ma and Pa.*

She had been in the woods only a short time when she felt her shoulders start to relax. It was cool in the shade of the trees, and quiet. Well, except for the few birds she heard, and the occasional angry chiding by a squirrel whose solitude she disturbed. No sign of the rumored bears or mountain lions either. Her pace was slow, but she'd expected that. When she found her first little creek, she paused briefly to drink deeply and eat the fresh apple she'd swiped from the kitchen. Then she pushed herself onward. She knew she had to put as much distance between herself and the house as she could, especially on this first day when she was fresher.

By the time it was too dark to see anymore, Ruby was utterly exhausted. For the past half hour or so she'd been tripping over stones and even small sticks, dragging her bad leg through the leaves and dirt. She collapsed against the base of a large oak tree, wrapping her shawl around herself like a blanket, and fell instantly asleep.

The next morning, Ruby realized her trip through the woods was going to take much longer than she'd figured it would. She was jolted awake by the loud cawing of a large black crow as it hopped among the branches overhead. As she sat up and stretched, Ruby realized something else. Her bum leg was throbbing in pain. Wishing she'd thought to bring along some liniment or aspirin, Ruby slowly stood, leaning against the tree. She'd have to keep her eyes peeled for a willow tree. Her mother had told her that chewing the bark worked as well as aspirin, and she figured she'd try anything at this point. She took a stale biscuit and a hard-boiled egg from her stash, hurriedly choking most of them down, and leaving a few crumbs of the biscuit on the ground for the crow.

Ruby didn't remember much of that day. It seemed to pass in a fog. She'd walk for as long as she could, then sit a spell, then walk some more. She knew her progress was pitifully slow, but it was all she could manage. Once again, when it was too dark to see, she collapsed at the base of a tree and fell instantly asleep.

The third day passed much like the second, except Ruby stopped well before dark, unable to go any farther. She had no idea how far she'd come, or how much farther she had to go to reach help. At that moment she was so exhausted and in so much pain, she wasn't sure she wouldn't welcome a visit by a bear or mountain lion. *Dying here would be better than going back, I guess.* Noting that her thoughts were turning maudlin, Ruby pulled out the last of the jerky and tried to eat it. After a few chews, she put it away, to save it for tomorrow. Again, she wrapped herself in her shawl and fell deeply asleep.

Eleven

MAY AND CYRUS

The rumble of thunder pulled Ruby from her sleep in the dim light of dawn. It wasn't raining yet, but she bet it soon would be. She quickly finished off the jerky she'd saved, and struggled to her feet. Leaning heavily on her walking stick, she started limping through the trees. A sudden painfully bright flash of light was followed by an ear-splitting boom. Ruby looked back and saw that lightning had cleaved one of the trees, the same tree she'd sheltered under that night. She watched as half of the tree fell away, revealing the tree's smoldering heartwood. *Well, don't that just beat all!* Shaking her head, she continued limping along as the sky opened up and a driving rain fell, making itself felt even under the trees. Ruby drew her shawl over her head and trudged on.

The storm lasted only a few hours, but by the time it stopped, Ruby was soaked to the bone. Even the last of the biscuits was a soggy mess when she pulled it out. Ruby leaned against a tree to rest, not sure she'd be able to get up again if she sat on the ground. She was beyond exhausted, needing food and proper rest in the worst way. Her mind felt stuffed with cotton wool, which was why it took her a while to realize what she was hearing. There it was again. Faint, but she was sure that was the moo of a cow. She laughed at herself, thinking she was hearing things that weren't real, but there it was again. Hope surging through her, Ruby headed in the direction of the faint sound, dragging her leg and hurrying as best she could.

Suddenly, the trees ended, and Ruby found herself at the edge of a large meadow. There was the cow she'd heard, in a crudely patched-together corral that was attached to a lean-to shed. More importantly as far as Ruby was concerned, on the far side of the meadow was a small cabin, smoke curling lazily out of the chimney. She saw an old pickup truck snugged up next to the cabin's side, and a large kitchen garden on the other side. With tears sliding down her cheeks, she struggled across the meadow toward the cabin. She was almost to the porch when the door was flung open and a grandmotherly-shaped black woman stepped out.

"You poh thing! What happened to you? You a mess – all wet and muddy." Not waiting for an answer, the woman turned back toward the house and called out, "Cyrus, bring me one of them ol' blankets from under the bed." She came down off the porch still talking to Ruby. "You look all done in, chil'. Let me he'p you up these steps. Where you come from?"

"Here you go, May. Wrap her in this." A thin white-haired black man came out onto the porch, carrying a worn blanket.

"Thank you, dear." May wrapped the blanket around Ruby, and led her into the cabin. Ruby clung to the woman, unable to stop crying, her relief was so great. To feel safe again was an almost frightening feeling.

"Help me, please," Ruby managed to choke out.

"Of course we will. Now you come on over here by the stove and warm up a bit while I get you somethin' hot to drink. When you feel more like yourself, you kin tell us what you doin' out here on you own an' so far from anythin'." Filling a chipped mug with hot coffee from the pot on the back of the wood-burning stove, May kept chattering at the girl, partly to give her time to compose herself, and partly due to May's strong mothering instincts.

"Here, let me take that for you." Cyrus reached out to take the mug from Ruby, noting how she flinched away from him. "Okay, you carry it. Sit on down here at the table, and tell us what's brought you to our doorstep lookin' so ill-used." He sat at the small table, gesturing for her to join him. May sat too, pulling her chair close to Ruby.

"Ill-used?" Ruby gave a bitter laugh. "Funny you should put it that way. I've been held against my will for almost two years now, just a couple of days' walk that way," and she gestured with her free hand. The other hand clutched the mug. Ruby hesitated, unsure how much to reveal to these people. Would they understand? Would they even believe her? Would they think she was a crazy woman? Or would they send her back? Taking a shuddering breath, she began at the beginning. "I was on a bus from Norfolk to Roanoke, goin' home, and I met a man …." By the time Ruby was finished telling her story, May had reached out and taken the girl's hand, offering what comfort she could. Ruby added, "It wasn't just Joe and Ray. There were lots of other fellas comin' by the place, even a sheriff. I need your help to get away and go home, back to Roanoke."

Cyrus shook his head. "Lordy, girl. Roanoke's a long ways north of here. You was plannin' to walk all that way? My, my. Not sure you woulda made it."

"I sure woulda tried! I can't go back. You do believe what I told you, don't you?" Ruby searched their faces, looking for some sign that they believed her.

May smiled at Ruby, tears welling in her eyes. "Course we believe you been through some real bad times, chil'. Now, time for you to get a little sleep while me and Cyrus figure out the best way to he'p you. First, you gotta get out of those wet clothes. Cyrus, you wait outside for me." Once the man left, May helped Ruby out of her sodden dress and into one of May's own nightgowns, tucking her under the quilts on the bed. "You sleep a while now, y' hear?" As May left, Ruby fell fast asleep, feeling safe and unburdened for the first time in a long while.

May joined Cyrus by the side of the corral. "What you thinkin'? You believe her?" he asked.

"I think so, but not fer sure. She believes what she tol' us, that's a fact. She's surely been mistreated … you saw how she jerked away from you in there … but …."

"You know who she meant by 'Joe and Ray', don't you?"

"That I do. That makes it a mite easier to accept her tale." May sighed heavily.

"Yeah. Joe's meaner than a snake, we know that for a fact, but to do what all she said … I swear I didn't think he were that lost. You think she's in her right mind?" Cyrus scratched his head in frustration.

"I just don' know. What we do now?"

51

"I think I go down to town and maybe talk to the sheriff. I can't believe he'd be mixed up in this mess." Cyrus gave May a quick kiss on the forehead and turned to leave. "Don't let on where I've gone – just say I went to get he'p. I'd hate for her to get scairt an' run again."

"I won't. Be careful an' hurry back." May walked Cyrus to the truck and watched as he negotiated the rutted track across the meadow. Not wanting to disturb Ruby, she walked slowly around the cabin to the garden. She had much to think about, and working in her garden always helped.

Twelve

BETRAYED

Through the open cabin door, Ruby could see that daylight was failing. She had slept for most of the day, only waking when May came in to start a stew for supper. The cold cornbread and buttermilk the woman had given Ruby to tide her over had tasted like ambrosia, and she tried not to wolf it down. Once May had the stew simmering on the back of the stove, they settled at the table to talk while they waited for Cyrus to return. After a bit, Ruby got quiet, her hands twisting in her lap.

"What's wrong, chil'?" May asked softly.

Ruby looked at her. "You don't believe me, do you? You think I'm touched in the head, don't you?"

"Of course I b'lieve you chil'. I can tell you been mistreated and all. It's just hard to b'lieve people'd be so mean to a girl like you."

"I swear it's the truth, every bit of it! I'll swear on the Good Book! I will!"

"Now don't go gettin' all het up. I've got more than a few years on you, chil', an' while I b'lieve most people's good, I've seen they don't always act like it. Turns my stomach, ya know?"

Ruby sighed, shoulders drooping as she sat forward. "I know. But everythin' I told you is true."

May reached over and patted her hand. "Cyrus should be back afore long. He went to get you some he'p and find out what he could. Fact I hear his old rattle-trap acomin' now," May rose and went to stand on the porch, Ruby trailing behind her. Cyrus pulled his truck up to the cabin, calling out a greeting as he got out. A familiar-looking sedan with an official seal on the driver's door came to a stop behind the truck. Ruby watched in horror as she got a good look at the man getting out of the sedan.

"What have you done? How could you do this to me?" Ruby whispered, her voice breaking. She turned to May, grabbing the woman's arms. "It's him! It's the sheriff, the one Joe owns. He's gonna kill me! Or worse, he'll take me back."

The sheriff slammed the car door, calling out as he approached the porch. "Now Miz Ruby, don't you go carryin' on so. There's no call to get so riled up. And you got no cause to worry May and Cyrus after they've been so kind to you." As he talked, Sheriff Atlee mounted the steps, coming to a stop in front of Ruby. "Time to go, girl."

When the sheriff reached out to grab Ruby's arm, she swung at him, knocking his hat from his head. He picked her up bodily and carried her to the car. Cyrus and May looked on helplessly as Ruby kicked and screamed, twisting in the sheriff's arms. "Gonna have to cuff you till you calm down," he said, pinning her to the car with his body as he fumbled with the handcuffs.

The click of the handcuffs around her wrists caused Ruby to freeze. She couldn't believe this was happening. As the sheriff shoved her into the back of his car, she fell heavily on her bum leg. She lay there shuddering, tears streaming down her face. The hope she'd known just a few short hours ago was gone, replaced by a numbness of mind and spirit like a dense fog.

"Sorry you had to see that, folks," the sheriff said, addressing Cyrus and May. "Y'all can see she's actin' a mite crazy right now. Don't worry. I'll take her back with me, and listen to her story. Probably put her on a bus to home, once she calms down." He took the hat May held out to him. "Thank you kindly, Miz May. Don't you be worryin' anymore about her. I'll take care of things from here."

As the sheriff drove off with Ruby in the back seat, May turned to Cyrus. "I hope you did the right thing, gettin' him involved. What if he really is what she said he was?"

"May, we've known that man for a long time. For a white man, he ain't half bad. You really think he'd do what she said? We gonna take the word of one slip of a girl, nigh on to hysterical to boot?"

"I know, but ...."

"We done the best we could for her. Now let it rest. What's for supper? I'm feelin' a mite hungry." Cyrus took May's hand, and they went into the cabin, closing the door on the fading light of the day.

Ruby braced herself as best she could in the backseat of the car, her mind a jumble of fear and anger. She remembered Sundays in the little church back home where she learned her prayers and tried to do what Ma told her was right. But right now, those prayers refused to come.

"They don't know you very well, do they?" Ruby asked softly.

It was quiet for so long she didn't think he was going to answer her. "Look, I don't expect you to understand this, but what happens at Joe's place ...

that whole deal … it's a separate part of my life. It doesn't affect who I really am. I'm a respectable man, a widow man. And I still take my Mama to church on Sunday. More important, I keep my town safe."

She snorted. "Safe? From the likes of Joe and Ray? Does your Mama know what you do there? About the whores and the payoffs?"

"You keep my Mama out of this!"

"You brought her up, not me. I reckon she'd bring down a little hellfire of her own on you if she ever found out what all you been doin'."

"I said, leave my Mama out of it 'fore you get me real mad. You won't like me riled up."

Ruby grunted. "I don't much like you when you're not riled up, either." After another long silence, she asked, "Why'd you tell them you were gonna put me on a bus home?"

"I know you think I'm lower than a snake's belly, but I really do care about these people. I needed to tell them somethin' they'd understand – I couldn't just throw you in the back of the car and light on out of there. May is too much of a motherly type – she'd have worried herself sick over you, halfway believin' your story. And then she'd have pestered me wantin' to know what happened to you. This way, she won't worry."

"Right. Gee, how kind of you. It had nothing to do with coverin' up for yourself, right? And come Sunday, you'll take your Mama to church and sit there all pious-like and feel good 'cause you kept May from worryin'. But you'll take me back to Joe and not feel a bit guilty for throwin' me back into hell? You really are a miserable excuse for a human being!"

"Maybe not as miserable as you think. They sent me out to hunt you down, you know. Joe and Ray didn't care if I brought you back alive or dead. I think they'd have preferred dead actually, so you couldn't never tell nobody about them."

"Or about you."

"Or about me. I should just kill you and dump you up here, but I can't make myself do that. Maybe for the same reasons you haven't poisoned Joe and Ray by now. It just wouldn't be right. I've taken bribes and looked the other way, I've whored some. But I draw the line at murder. That's goin' too far."

"They wanted you to kill me?"

"As I recollect, Joe allowed as how that'd be the best solution for everybody."

"'Except me.'" Ruby took a shaky breath. "If you take me back to them, they'll most likely kill me anyway. You know that's true."

"If I don't take you back … I just can't risk crossin' those guys."

"So you're just gonna take me back? You're just gonna wash your hands of me and let them do what they want? I was right – you are a miserable excuse for a human being."

"Girl, you need to remember, there ain't nobody here now but just the two of us, so you better watch your mouth."

"Whatcha gonna do? Rape me – you already done that. Beat me? That'd be new from you, but I'm used to it from Joe."

"You just keep on bumpin' your gums. I ain't gonna do nothin' to you. You're gonna spend the night in a jail cell, and I'll take you back up the mountain tomorrow. I'm thinkin' Joe's gonna be none too pleased with you. The beatings you had from him before? This one's gonna be worse, so much worse. You just think on that now."

Thirteen

RETURNED TO HELL

Spending the night in a cell was a lowering experience for Ruby, further eroding her sense of who she was, of her value. She didn't sleep much, just stared at the stained ceiling over the bunk and tried not to think of what the morning would bring. Dawn was just beginning to lighten the sky when the sheriff brought her a mug of coffee.

"Here. Be quick about it. I need to get you to Joe and get back to town 'fore everybody's up and about." He turned to go.

"You don't have to take me back, you know," she pleaded.

"I think I do," he replied without turning to look at her.

"You could just put me on a bus. You told May you were gonna do that. If anybody ever asks, you could say that's what you did."

Turning back to her, he paused, then shook his head. "I can't do that. I'm gonna take you back to Joe, but that's the last favor I'll be doin' for him. I'm done." Unlocking the cell door, he gestured for her to come out. "Let's go."

Hurriedly, Ruby gulped down the last of the bitter coffee, setting the mug carefully on the floor. "Please …. Please, Sheriff. You know Joe and Ray. They're gonna kill me, sure as I'm standin' here. You got hooked up with them, and you've done some pretty bad things, but do you really want to be party to murder? That's what it'll be if you take me back."

The sheriff just shook his head and again gestured for her to come out. "Let's go," he repeated.

Ruby tried one last time. "Please. I'm beggin' you- don't take me back. My life is in your hands. You got a lot to atone for. Don't add murder to it."

His hand tightly gripping her arm, he led her outside to his car parked in the alley behind the station. She pulled at his grip, opening her mouth to scream for help. "None of that now," and he shook her. "Just get in." He opened the back door of the car and pushed her in.

Instead of immediately starting the car, Atlee sat in silence, head lowered, hands on the wheel. As if coming to a decision, he turned in his seat to look back at Ruby. "If I put you on a bus headin' north, if I do that, you gotta promise me somethin'. You gotta promise me you won't ever say a word about me, about my helpin' out Joe and Ray, about what I did to you. I don't care what you say about Joe and Ray, but nothin' about me."

"I promise! Oh, yes, I promise." Ruby leaned back against the seat, weak with the joy rushing through her.

Atlee looked at her, and slowly shook his head. "I can't believe I'm doin' this, but ... I believe you. You're an odd woman, Ruby, but you understand honor more than most folks. I can't believe I'm doin' this!" He repeated. Atlee turned and started the car. He'd gone about ten feet, when another car pulled into the alley in front of him.

Ruby cried out, "No!" as Joe got out of the car.

"Damn!" Atlee turned back to her. "I really was goin' to put you on that bus. Like you said, it might have helped make up for some of what I've done. I'm sorry, girl." With that, he turned off the car and got out, opening Ruby's door and pulling her out.

"I found somethin' of yours," the sheriff said pushing her forward.

"Aces, sheriff, aces!" Never taking his eyes off the sheriff, Joe casually backhanded Ruby, and she fell to the ground. "You wanna come up to the house and enjoy yourself? We just brought back a new one."

"No. I'm done, Joe. Catchin' this one is the last thing I'm gonna do for you. I won't blow the whistle on you, but ... I'm done."

"What you mean 'you're done'? I own you, or did you forget that little detail? You can't just walk away."

"You're wrong about that. I won't be back out there." Atlee gestured to Ruby. "And I ain't gonna fetch nobody for you again."

Joe advanced toward Atlee. "You gonna blow the whistle on us?"

"Said I wouldn't. But it works both ways; you blow the whistle on me, I blow it on you. I'm done."

Joe glared at him. "Maybe you are, and maybe you ain't. I'm guessin' you'll be back, 'cause flesh is weak. Time will tell. Anyway, thanks for catchin' her. Dump her in my trunk and I'll be off."

Pulling up in front of the house, Joe honked. Coming around to the back, he opened the trunk and pulled Ruby out. She didn't know why it surprised her that the old house looked the same. She figured it should have sprouted gargoyles or be painted black to reflect what went on there. Ray came out of the house, followed by a slender girl Ruby didn't recognize. Ray motioned for her to stay on the porch, as he came down the steps and met Joe and Ruby halfway across the yard.

"So, the sheriff came through, huh? She looks a little worse for wear, doesn't she?" Ray looked her up and down.

"You try ridin' in a trunk sometime and see how you turn out!" Ruby spat out at him.

Ray backhanded her. "Watch your mouth, Gimp!"

Joe looked down at Ruby where she lay on the ground. "Get up!" She struggled to her feet, lunging at him as she did. He easily sidestepped her and knocked her down again. "Oh, I don't think so. Get up, I said!" To the girl on the porch he said, "You pay attention now. This is how I deal with a troublemaker. You watch and learn somethin'." To Ruby he said, "You shoulda known better … disobeyin' me … runnin' away like that. Now you gotta pay for that. Ray, come hold her up."

"Sure, Joe."

For what seemed like an eternity to Ruby, Joe slammed his fists into her body, backhanding her, even kicking at her legs. All the while, Ray held her in place for his brother. Finally, his anger spent, Joe signaled to Ray to let her drop.

"You," he yelled to the girl on the porch. "Come here." As she approached, he gestured to Ruby's still form. "Get her to the hen house, and then come find me. This has got me all riled up, and I'm thinkin' you can help me with that." Joe grunted, wiped his bloody hands on his pants, and headed toward the house.

Ray bent down to help the girl lift an unconscious Ruby off the ground. Joe looked back. "Whatcha doin', Ray? I told the new girl to do that."

"True. Be quicker if I do it though." He took Ruby from the girl. "This one can even go with you now instead of later."

"Hmm." Joe threw a key on a lanyard at Ray. "Here. Make sure you lock her in."

As gently as he could, Ray deposited Ruby on her bunk. A quick inventory of her injuries revealed a couple of broken ribs, severe bruising on her legs, several smaller bruises and cuts, and a handful of deeper cuts to her face. Both eyes were swollen shut and already beginning to blacken. "It's a shame, but

… you knew better. Surprised he didn't kill you. Next time he will, you know," Ray said softly. He drew a thin blanket over her and left, locking the new padlock on the door after him.

Several hours later, Ruby was faintly aware of the sound of the door opening. Someone stumbled in, and the door slammed shut again. A lantern hissed as it was lit. She felt the gentle pressure of a hand on her forehead.

"You poor thing! I don't know much doctorin' so I don't know how much help I can be, but I can at least wash you off some." Ruby heard the sound of the pump being worked, and then the voice came back closer. "My name's Della, by the way. They told me not to use it here, but I thought you should know." With that, Della began gently washing away the blood from Ruby's body. First her face, then her arms and legs, and finally … "Ruby, I'm gonna have to take off your dress to check the rest of you, okay?" Not waiting for a reply, she unbuttoned the front of the dress, and proceeded to, ever so gently, wipe Ruby down. By the time she was done, Della was trembling. She had never seen someone beaten so badly. "I wish I had some mercurochrome for your cuts. We'll just have to keep them clean and hope for the best. You sleep now." Della dumped the basin of bloody water down the cracked sink in the corner.

She blew out the lamp, and climbed into a bunk near Ruby. She was not surprised when sleep was slow to come that night.

Fourteen

MAY GOES TO ROANOKE

August 1933
Roanoke, Virginia

It had been two weeks since the sheriff took Ruby away. Two weeks in which May couldn't stop thinking about the girl, wondering if she was alright, if she'd made it home yet. As it came time for her yearly trip to visit her sister, Ada, in Roanoke, May decided she would try to check on the girl while she was there.

"How you plannin' to do that?" Cyrus wanted to know.

"Well, we never got her last name, so I can't find her folks to ask. I guess I'll just ask the sheriff there if he knows anythin'. Mebbe he can tell me somethin'. Worth a try," May responded.

"If it makes you rest easy, then do it. Just don't 'spect too much."

"I know. But I gotta try."

May boarded the Greyhound from Dalton to Roanoke the next morning, making her way to a seat in the rear of the bus. She asked the driver if he'd seen Ruby, but he was new to the route, so that was a dead end. May spent the next two weeks catching up with Ada about what had happened to them over the past year. Ada lived in a small house in Roanoke proper, and she loved to joke that she was the city mouse to May's country mouse. Much chicory coffee was drunk, and the knitting needles clacked constantly, as the sisters caught up on each other's lives. Ada was very interested in May's tale about Ruby, and agreed that they should go see the sheriff before May returned home. Maybe he knew something about the girl, and could put May's mind at ease.

On the last day of May's visit, she and Ada ventured into the sheriff's office in downtown Roanoke. As they waited their turn, May couldn't help but notice the man talking to the sheriff. He seemed agitated.

"Sheriff Carter, we wanted to check and see if you'd heard anything. She couldn't have just vanished like that," the man said.

"I'm sorry, Mr. Malcolm, but there's been no news. You know I'd let you know if there was."

"It's just …" the man paused, his shoulders slumping. "Come on, Lida, let's head on home." The man took the arm of the woman standing next to him and began to walk out with her.

May turned to watch them walk past. Something caused her to call out, "Excuse me, sir. You mebbe lookin' for a white girl named Ruby? Red hair an' freckles? 'Bout my height?"

The man stopped in his tracks, and the woman spun to face May. "What do you know about my girl? Have you seen her? Please … tell me," she pleaded tearfully.

Sheriff Carter, recognizing that the lobby of the station was no place for this conversation, ushered them all into his office. "I don' know much, but I seen her. She showed up on my doorstep up in the hills a ways from here. She was soppin' wet from some rain we had, and she tol' me and my Cyrus she'd run away from someplace. Cyrus fetched the sheriff to he'p her out. Last I saw of her, the sheriff was takin' her down to Dalton. Said he was gonna put her on a bus. If anybody knows what happened after that, I guess he do," ended May.

"Carter, can you call him?" Ruby's mother asked the sheriff.

"Let's see what he knows," Carter said, reaching for the phone on his desk. "Millie, put me through to the sheriff down in Dalton. Yeah, I'll hold." After about five minutes, Cade Atlee, the sheriff in Dalton, came on the line, and Carter explained why he was calling. "Cade, we're just wantin' to know when you last saw her, and if she was alright."

"Well, sure. I felt kinda sorry for her. I put her on a bus headin' for Roanoke the next morning. That's the last I saw of her. She was okay when she left here. That's all I know."

"Thanks. If you see her again, would you please call me? She never got here, and her folks are mighty worried about her."

"Sure, Sheriff. Will do," and Sheriff Atlee hung up.

Carter relayed the information, or the lack of it, to the four gathered in his office. There was a moment of thoughtful silence, and then Ruby's father asked, "Can we ask the bus driver on the route from Dalton to Roanoke? Maybe he remembers her."

"I already asked on the trip up here," May said. "The driver's new, and he said he didn't recollect seein' her. I'm sorry I couldn't he'p you more."

"At least we know she was alive a few weeks ago. That's more hope than we had before, so thank you for that." Ruby's father shook May's hand as she and Ada stood to leave.

Back on the sidewalk, Ada looked at May. "Times like this I regret I'm a teetotaler. "

"Me too, Sister. Me too."

Fifteen

LITTLE ACTS OF RESISTANCE

January 1934

New Year's Day, 1934, dawned bitterly cold. Too cold to snow, though the air was heavy with the smell of it. Ruby trudged her way across the yard to the big house, using the crude walking stick she'd come to depend on. Her right leg, the one broken in her fall down the stairs, had never healed right to start with. It had been re-injured when Joe viciously beat her, and now it pained her constantly. The cold just made it worse. Eyeing the gray sky, Ruby hoped the snow would hold off until Ray got back with the supplies. She could care less if he died in a fiery crash off the side of the mountain, but she did want the flour and apples he'd gone to get. Couldn't make the pies without those. Thinking about apple pies made Ruby think of Della who had loved her pies. She wondered how Della was faring. Ruby didn't expect to ever hear from her again, but she hoped the girl had made it out.

After the beating back in July, it had taken Ruby a good two months to heal up. Gradually, as the ribs healed, she was able to breathe without pain. The bruises faded and the cuts healed, though one of the cuts on her face left a scar behind, across most of her right cheek where Joe's ring had cut her. At first the scar horrified her, and she went out of her way to avoid mirrors. But after a while, Ruby came to think of it as her badge of courage. It reminded her of her failed escape attempt, but it also reminded her that she had been strong enough, courageous enough, to try. That's what she chose to focus on.

If it had not been for Della, Ruby was sure she would have died. All through the first few weeks after the beating, when Ruby was barely aware of her surroundings, Della nursed her as best she could, and brought her food – soup and broth at first, and then more as she was able to eat. The long cut on her right cheek had gotten infected, hence the scar, but luckily that was the only one to fester.

Somehow, Ray was able to convince Joe to keep Della at the place so she could take care of Ruby, and fill in for her until she was back on her feet. For that, Ruby was grateful. Della would come back to the hen house in the evening, bringing Ruby food, and they'd talk a while until one or the other of them fell asleep.

"Della, you know they're gonna sell you on soon, right? As soon as they think I can do what's needed here, they'll do it."

"Yeah, I know. Joe said somethin' like that yesterday." Della was quiet for a minute. "It scares me, a lot. But at least I'll be out of here. You won't."

"Don't you worry 'bout me. I don't know how, I don't know when, but someday I'll be quit of this place. You can count on that."

"I believe you will. You're good people, Ruby. Don't you forget that."

"I don't feel 'specially good, not with all the hate I feel inside. Della, I'd have died if it weren't for you. I think Joe intended that."

"Maybe he did. But we didn't let him win that one," and Della grinned at Ruby before blowing out the lamp.

All the next day, Ruby thought about what Della had said, about scoring a win against Joe and Ray. The more she thought about it, the more she liked it. She resolved, from here on out, to 'win' as often as she could, no matter how small the win was. The occasional burned supper, no biscuits with a meal because there was no flour, and unwashed sheets –

little things, normal things, but something to make life a little less comfortable for Joe and Ray, to gum up the works a bit. She would have to be careful so they didn't figure out what she was doing, but it would be almost fun. And then she thought of something else she could do, not for herself, but for the girls who passed through. That evening she shared her idea with Della.

"Look, I want to do something to help you. And I thought of something. It's not much, but …. Promise me, wherever you end up, no matter how long it takes, run away from there. If you can get to my folks' farm, I know they'll take you in. They're good people. They'll help you get back on your feet, and even help you get home if you want. I know they will." Ruby told her how to find the farm outside of Roanoke.

"I'll try. If I get there, what should I tell them about you?"

"Just that I'm alive, and I love them. That's good enough. The rest would just hurt them too much." And Ruby rolled over to face the wall, feigning sleep.

Within a fortnight, Della was gone. Ruby had to endure three days locked in the hen house while

Joe and Ray drove her away. Luckily, they'd allowed Ruby to gather up a stash of food and a large pitcher of water before they locked her in. In an odd way, she almost enjoyed the solitude.

The men returned on the third day, bringing with them a young terrified girl. Joe immediately proceeded to rape her and begin her 'training'.

"We'll be needin' supper in a bit," Ray said when he unlocked the door, letting her out. "You'd best get on it."

That night, the creamed chipped beef was a little watery, and the toast was a bit burnt. The lima beans were perfect, though.

Sixteen

THE JOURNAL IS BEGUN

February 1934

It was fun at first, finding little ways to get back at the men. Ruby thought to herself. *The meals a little off, the dishes not as clean as could be, dirt in the corners, moving a little slower. I even smiled at something Ray said one night, though I wanted to spit at him. I almost laughed at the look on Joe's face. He was so confused. Good! Let him think I'm losing it, that I'm going crazy – It makes him underestimate me. All that was fun at first, but not so much now. I want to do more, but I haven't hit on what yet. Have to be so, so careful.*

There were two girls at the place now. And Ruby. But she figured she didn't count as much more than the housekeeper. Ray had gone down to Dalton again, and returned with not just the much needed supplies, but another young thing. This girl was small, like Mary had been, and Ruby was afraid for her. She knew she'd never forget the sight of Mary's lifeless hand seeming to wave at her as Joe carried the body into the woods. She promised herself that would never happen again, if she could help it.

Two weeks passed, and Ruby did her best to make life at least bearable for the two girls. The infrequent casual beatings and continued 'training' aside, both of the girls seemed to be coping with their new reality. At night, there were tears and long whispered conversations, but during the day, they faced the men calmly. It puzzled Ruby at first, until one night, the oldest of the girls explained.

"We saw what you do to get back at them, all the little things. And we wanted to do somethin' too. This is our way of resistin' them. It confuses them when we don't put up a fight. It keeps them off kilter."

"If you noticed … do you think they have?" Ruby was suddenly very worried.

"No. Or at least not that you're doin' it on purpose. Ray even said he thinks you're not all there since Joe beat you so bad," the younger girl replied.

"Just play it safe. I don't think I could take it if they figure out what you're doin'. You could end up like me, or worse, like Mary."

"Who's Mary? What happened to her?"

When Ruby finished explaining, there were fresh tears on all their cheeks. They grieved for the girl, and it was a harsh reality that it could just as easily happen to them.

"I was gonna wait till right before you leave here to tell you this, but I think you could stand to know this now. My folks have a farm outside of Roanoke ..." and Ruby told them what she'd told Della. "If you can get there ...."

"We'll try. We will surely try," the older girl assured her.

The next day, as Ruby was adding to the list of needed supplies for Ray to eventually pick up in town, she had a sudden idea. Looking at her hand clutching the stub of the pencil as she wrote 'baking powder' on the small pad of paper, she thought of another way she could fight back. She'd start a journal, a very secret journal. And she'd write down what happened here. Everything. Her story and Mary's, and well ... everything. She'd have to be very, very careful though. If Joe or Ray saw it, found out what she was doing, Ruby just knew she'd end up buried alongside Mary in the woods.

I'll use what paper I can scrounge up. I'll hide it so they can't find it. Someday ... someday, maybe I can use it to bring them down, to bring justice for all these girls.

80

And so, Ruby began her journal, tearing out the last page of the pad she was using that day, folding it, and hiding it in her apron pocket. She found another pencil stub in one of the kitchen drawers, and it joined the piece of paper in her pocket. That night, after the girls were asleep, Ruby wrapped herself in her blanket and huddled near the pot-bellied stove that warmed the hen house. Opening the stove door a crack, she used that dim light as she began to write, her handwriting small and cramped, her grammar careless.

> *They musn't know I keep this journal. If Joe found out he'd beat me or worse. And here there is a lot of worse. Don't know if anybody will ever see this and know, but I hope they will and I must write what goes on here. People need to know. So much fear, so much sadness, so much pain. I'll hide this and write when I can. I was on my way home when Ray stole me from the bus in Roanoke. He seemed like nice man. Took me to his brother and they raped me and hurt me. Now I'm a cripple and they keep me here to work for them. I don't even know where 'here' is. Somewhere in the mountains, a long ways from Roanoke, and near Dalton.*

That night, Ruby hid her scrap of paper under her thin mattress, but she knew that wouldn't be safe enough. She needed someplace nobody would ever think to look. And it had to be in the hen house – too dangerous otherwise. The next morning, in the dim light filtering through the small window, Ruby looked around the hen house. Not much to see, and even less in the way of hiding places. Bunk beds – all solid. Floor boards – none loose. Rafters – too exposed. Then she remembered something. There was a piece of trim alongside the door that was loose. She'd already had to nail it back up a couple of times. Maybe that would work. As the other girls began to stir, Ruby knelt down by the door, testing the trim. There! The loose piece came off in her hand. There behind it was a small opening, maybe four inches by two inches. Good enough to use. Securing the piece of trim back where it belonged, she wrapped her threadbare sweater tightly about her, and waited for Ray to unlock the door so she could head to the big house to start breakfast. She felt a little bit brighter, even a little hopeful that morning. She still hated the men fiercely. She still hated her situation and what she had to do. But now, she felt a glimmer of peace too.

Seventeen

AN ATTEMPTED POISONING

March 1934

March came in like a lion that year. There might have only been eight inches of snow on the ground, but the temperature never made it over freezing. And at night, temperatures well below freezing combined with gusty winds to make it brutal. Joe and Ray had been gone almost a week now. They left the night before the storm hit, taking the two girls down the mountain with them, and locking Ruby in the hen house. So far her stash of food had held out, but there was only enough wood for one more night. After that ... well, Ruby didn't want to think about how cold it would get. *Maybe I'll freeze to death – that'd be one way to be free of here. With my luck though, I'd probably just get real sick*, Ruby thought as she dozed off out of boredom.

It seemed like just seconds later when Ruby jolted awake, hearing car doors slamming in the yard. She heard shouting and what sounded like a scuffle, and then the sound of the key turning in the lock. The door was flung open, and Joe and Ray shoved two girls into the hen house, slamming the door behind them. Through the door, Ruby heard Joe yell, "Explain things to them. We'll be back for them as soon as we get some heat goin' in the house."

"What is this place?" asked one of the girls, looking around and frowning.

The other girl answered, "It's our prison, you nitwit." She had the makings of a shiner evident around one eye. Hands on her hips, she turned to glare at Ruby. "Bet you're the warden, too."

Ruby slowly stood from where she'd been sitting on her bunk. "You're right, this is your new prison, or as close to that as can be. But I'm not your warden. Far from it. I'm in the same boat as you are. But I've been here nigh unto two years now, and I've learned a few things the hard way. Things you need to know to survive this place. Sit. Let's talk – we don't have much time." The two girls reluctantly sat on the bunk opposite Ruby as she struggled to explain their new reality to them. "You struggle, you get hurt. You don't struggle ... well, sometimes you get hurt then too," she concluded. They stared at her, eyes round with fear and anger, as they tried to take in what she'd told them to expect.

"How can they ... I mean, that's just evil," Tilda whispered.

Jean shook her head, wincing as her hair brushed against her bruised cheek. "There's lots of evil out there, honey. If this is your first time meetin' up with it, then you've been real lucky." Looking at Ruby, she said, "I guess what you're sayin' makes sense, but I can't promise I won't fight 'em. The Good Book says the meek will inherit the earth, but there's little meek in me."

A short time later, the men came to collect the girls and take them up to the house. "You," Ray called to Ruby over his shoulder. "Get started on supper. We're gonna be real hungry 'fore too long." With a sigh, Ruby rose from her bunk and trudged behind the group through the snow to the house.

The new girls had been there just over a week, and things had not gone smoothly. As Jean said, there was little meek about her. When she wasn't riling up Joe and Ray, she was squabbling with Tilda or Ruby.

> *Today was not a good day. Jean went off the rails, yelling at me to quit bossing her around, and to stop lording 'my position' over her. I'd have laughed if it weren't so sad. Not sure what she thinks 'my position' here is, but it's not any better than hers. In*

fact, it's worse. She will leave here, and I won't. And bossing her around? I'm just trying to help her survive this place with a few less slaps and a few less beatings. Guess I have to leave her be, but it pains me.

As Jean became more distant, Tilda attached herself to Ruby like a shadow. Whenever she could, she stayed by Ruby's side, helping her with the housekeeping and cooking. Ruby was grateful for the girl's company, even knowing it wouldn't last long. As contentious as Jean had become, Ruby was betting this pair of girls would be gone soon. In fact, just two days later, Ray took Jean along with him on his run down the mountain for supplies. He returned without her, and Ruby overheard him telling his brother that he'd found someone to take her.

Can't say I'm sorry Jean's gone. She was always arguing with me and Tilda. She'd take more than her fair share at supper, and then not pull her weight with the chores. I guess she defied Joe one too many times, and he had Ray sell her on quick like. At least I hope he sold her, and she didn't end up like Mary. I wish her well, wherever she is, but if she doesn't change some, things will be rough for her.

Tilda and Ruby were just putting away the last of the supper dishes when Joe burst into the kitchen. He grabbed Ruby by the upper arms and threw her against the wall. "What did you put in those taters?" he yelled.

Ruby slid to the floor. "What? Nothin'! Just … just taters, like usual," she stammered out in confusion.

"You lyin' bitch! That were so, then Ray wouldn't be pukin' right now." Joe yanked Ruby off the floor, backhanding her. "Now, tell me what you did. What'd you put in the taters?"

"Nothin'!" repeated Ruby, gasping as he squeezed her throat with one hand.

Her denial made Joe even madder. "What. Did. You. Put. In. The. Taters?" he yelled, every word punctuated by a stinging slap.

Tilda flung herself on Joe, grabbing his arm. "It was me! It was me, not her. I'm the one put somethin' in the taters. Was me."

Joe let go of Ruby, turning his attention to the girl who was now backing up across the kitchen. "What was it?" he ground out, pinning Tilda to the wall, his hand now on her throat.

"Just some spices like my Ma taught me. To make 'em not so borin'."

"Then why is Ray feelin' so poorly now, and pukin'?"

A terrified Tilda quivered in his grasp. "Don't know. Mebbe the spices were off, or mebbe they just didn't agree with him."

In an effort to calm the situation, Ruby spoke up. "Show me what you used."

When Joe loosened his grip and shoved her across the kitchen, Tilda grabbed two McCormick spice tins off the shelf over the stove. "These. I used these," she cried out, holding the tins out.

Ruby took them from the girl and sniffed them. "They smell okay to me. Musta just been they didn't sit well with him."

"You both stay right here. I'm gonna check on Ray."

After Joe stepped out, Ruby turned a teary-eyed Tilda to face her. "What did you really use?"

"Just those, like I said."

"Uh, uh. I know spices, and I know herbs." Ruby handed the tins back to Tilda. "A little sage and a little red pepper wouldn't cause an upset gut like that. What did you really use? And for the love of God, why?"

"I wanted them both to die!" Tilda hissed at Ruby. "Or get sick 'nuf we could steal the car and get away from here." She threw the tins across the room. "You wouldn't do anything, so I figured I would. I just wanted them dead."

"Yeah, that's what I figured," Joe growled from the doorway.

Tilda spun and tried to make it to the back door, but she crashed into Ruby and they went down in a heap. "I hate you, too! I hate you, too," she sobbed at Ruby.

Joe yanked her up by her arm, and again pinned her to the wall. "What. Did. You. Use?" Joe yelled in her face, tightening his hand around her throat.

"Just some weeds from the yard," she whispered around his grip.

Not loosening his hold on Tilda, Joe turned to Ruby. "You know what's growin' out there. Anythin' that'll kill Ray?"

"What'd it look like?" Ruby asked Tilda.

"Not tellin' ya!" the girl struggled against Joe's hold.

"Tell me. You're in big trouble, I won't lie. Don't make it worse," pleaded Ruby.

"It was that fuzzy lookin' bush by the kitchen door. With the pale blue flowers." Tears trickled down her cheeks. "Please, Sir. Let me go. I'll be good."

"Sounds like pukeweed to me." Ruby shook her head. "Make you sick, but won't kill you."

Tilda began to cry in earnest. "Please ... I won't do anythin' like that again. I promise. I'll be good. I just wanted to get out of here."

"Oh, you're gonna get out of here, alright. You," he said, addressing Ruby, "You finish up in here and beat feet out to the hen house. No funny business, y'hear?" Ruby nodded, eyes downcast. Joe started out the front door, dragging Tilda along as she screamed and tried to get free. He yelled out, "Ray, if you're done pukin', join us in the barn. We gotta teach this girl what happens to folks who try somethin'."

Ruby watched out the kitchen window as Joe dragged a struggling Tilda across the yard, while Ray staggered along, a ways behind them. She gasped when she saw the girl bite down hard on Joe's arm.

"Bitch!" Joe roared, felling her with a punch. He flung the girl's limp body over his shoulder and stumbled on into the barn.

Ruby laid her hand on the cool glass of the window. *Ah, Tilda, you can't hate me anymore than I hate myself because I can't get you out of this mess you made. If you'd just asked me, I'd have told you messing with the food wouldn't work. Or maybe I might have overcome my scruples about killing somebody, especially them, and showed you how to do it right. Now ... you poor thing! All I can do is hope I can patch you up in the morning. At least you drew blood. Maybe we'll all get lucky and it'll fester. We can hope.* Ruby headed out the kitchen door, across the yard to the hen house, shoulders slumped, dragging her bad leg.

The next morning, as Ruby was making coffee, Ray came downstairs, whistling. "Mornin'," he called out. "Coffee ready yet?"

"Almost," Ruby replied, not looking at him.

"Bring me a cup when it is. Oh, and by the way, Tilda's gone, so you don't have to worry 'bout her now."

Ruby just stared at his back as he calmly walked across the hallway into the living room. *Just like that?* She thought. *She's 'gone'? Bet they killed her and she's buried out next to Mary now. God, I hate them!* She had to wait for her hands to stop shaking before she could pour the coffee and take it to him.

Eighteen

DELLA ARRIVES AT THE FARM

March 1934
Roanoke, Virginia

As Lida gently kneaded the biscuit dough, her thoughts returned again to her daughter, Ruby. It had been almost a year and a half since her baby girl had disappeared. Oh, she knew Ruby was all grown up and not her baby anymore, but in her book, that's how all mothers thought of their children, no matter how old they got. It shouldn't have been possible for someone to simply vanish, but that's what seemed to have happened.

Lida had read and re-read the letter she'd gotten from Ruby saying she'd lost her job and she'd be coming home, to the farm, to stay a while until things got better. Though she was sorry that her daughter had lost the job she loved so much, Lida had been looking forward to having the girl back with them. She'd always worried about Ruby living 'out there', away from the farm and the family. Seems she was right to worry, and now she could only grieve and pray that her daughter was okay somewhere out there and would return someday. With a deep sigh, Lida slid the pan of biscuits into the oven and wiped her hands on her apron.

The knock on the door startled her. Figuring it was her husband, Tom, knocking because his hands were full of wood for the house, she called out, "Keep your shirt on there, mister. I'm acomin'." She flung open the door to find a startled-looking young woman, hand raised, preparing to knock again. "Oh! Sorry, I thought it was my Tom. We don't get many callers out here. You lost?"

"I hope not. My name's Della. I'm sure hopin' you're Ruby's mother 'cause she sent me to …"

Lida pulled Della into the house, interrupting what she'd been going to say. "You know my Ruby? Where is she? What's happened to her? Is she with you?" Lida looked past Della, out into the dusk-filled yard.

"I wish she was with me! She was a good friend to me, and I'll gladly tell you what I know."

Still clasping Della's hands, Lida seemed to gather herself. "Wait. Let me get her Pa in here so you can tell it once. He's been sick with worry too." Going out onto the porch, she yelled for her husband. "Thomas! Come quick! There's news of Ruby."

Within minutes, Lida and Tom were seated with Della around the kitchen table, and Della began.

"She told me, if I could ever escape, I should come here. She wanted me to tell you that she's alive, and that she loves you both very much."

"But why isn't she with you?" Lida asked, tears gathering in her eyes.

Tom frowned. "Escape what? What happened?"

Della rubbed tiredly at her face, and stared at the table top for a minute before she continued. "That was all she wanted me to say, but … I figure she wanted to be the one to tell you the rest, if … if she can escape and make it back here. It's pretty awful."

Tom shifted in his chair. "Look, Della … that's right, isn't it?" At Della's nod, he continued, "Della, we love our girl. Don't reckon anything will change that. We've been sick with worry about her. Please, tell us what you know."

With a yelp, Lida jumped up to snatch the pan of now half-burnt biscuits from the oven. She dumped them in the sink and sat back down. "I'll deal with that later. What you got to say is more important than some biscuits."

So Della began to speak. Slowly at first, with many pauses, she told Ruby's parents about what she knew had happened to their daughter. Dusk deepened into dark. Lamps were lit. Strong coffee left over from the morning filled their mugs.

Finally, drained, Della ended. "She was my friend, my rock when things were grim for both of us. She made me promise to try to get away and come here. She said you'd take me in and help me. I don't expect you to do that, but I needed to come here and let you know she's alive."

"What about your family? Don't you want to go back to them?" Tom asked.

Della shook her head. "None to go back to. The only one left is my older brother, Edwin, and the last I heard he was ridin; the rails, hopin' to get out to California. I guess he figured he could make it out there. Don't know how I'd get hold of him anymore."

Lida stood, gripping the edge of the table with her hands. "I won't pretend you haven't shaken us bad. My mind just doesn't want to think about my baby girl goin' through what you described. I just ... don't know what to do about it."

"Well, for starters," said Tom getting up from his chair, "we'll think on it overnight. I'm plannin' to go see the sheriff down in Roanoke tomorrow and let him know about this. Appreciate it if you'd come along, Della." She nodded, and he continued. "And of course, we'll take you in and help you! You can stay with us as long as you like, and … Oh, dear …" he stammered to a halt as Della burst into tears.

Lida gathered the sobbing girl into her arms. "It's okay now, darlin'. You're safe and you're home with us now. It's okay." She rocked Della back and forth a bit until the girl's crying stopped. "Tom, you go get us a load of wood, while I see to makin' a new batch of biscuits to go with the stew. Can't believe I let those ones burn like that! Haven't done that since I was a slip of a girl."

Lida bustled about the kitchen, making biscuits and heating up the stew, all the while regaling Della with stories about Ruby growing up. It wasn't long before Tom returned, and they sat down to a simple, hearty supper.

That night, as Della drifted off to sleep in Ruby's small bedroom, she could hear the rumble of Ruby's parents discussing what she'd told them. She hoped Ruby would forgive her for what she'd shared with them. She knew it hurt them to know that their daughter had been raped and beaten, and that she was still trapped in that situation. But she felt she owed them honesty. Maybe now they could all start to heal, and maybe now help would be forthcoming for Ruby.

"What'd ya think, Sheriff Carter? Will this help find our girl?" Tom asked the sheriff the next morning. In Roanoke, Della had told the sheriff what she knew.

"Maybe. All depends. Della, do you remember any landmarks that could help us pinpoint where this house is?" Carter asked.

"Anytime we were in the car, they'd cover our heads with flour sacks so we couldn't see where we were. I remember some smooth roads and a lot of really rough ones, but that's about all."

"What about 'round the house?"

"Lots of trees. Up in the hills. But nothin' that stood out."

"Okay. What about the men's names? There are lots of Joes and Rays in the mountains round about these parts. Did you ever hear a last name? Or maybe see it on some mail even?"

"Wish I had! They were real careful to hide all that." Della paused, thinking. "But maybe I just remembered somethin' that might help. One time, Ruby said she thought we were near someplace called 'Dalton'. But she never did say why she thought that."

The sheriff stood, coming around his desk. "Della, you may not think so, but you've been a big help. You've given Tom and Lida hope, for starters." Shaking hands with Tom, he added, "Tom, I'll let you know if anythin' comes of what Della's told me."

Sheriff Carter, hands clasped behind his head, leaned back in his chair and stared at the ceiling, lost in thought. This was the second time Dalton had come up in connection with Ruby's disappearance. That both puzzled and concerned him. He reached for the phone to call Sheriff Atlee in Dalton, hoping that the man had heard something since the last time they'd talked.

Cade Atlee listened to Carter's new information, and promised to look into it. "Names were Joe and Ray? Any last name? Lots of Joes and Rays in these mountains, y'know."

"That's what I told them. Just see what you can find out, okay? Let me know, Cade."

"Sure, will do." After he hung up with Carter, Atlee sat looking at the phone. A couple of months ago, he would have made a run out to Joe's house to let him know about the call. But not now. He'd told Joe, in no uncertain terms, that he was done being part of the operation at the house. He wouldn't be going out there again, not to warn them, not to arrest them, and not to enjoy himself with the girls. He wished he'd been able to put the girl on a bus, but when Joe showed up to check on his progress looking for her, that was no longer an option. What was done, was done.

Joe and Ray had been making and selling moonshine for a long while, as Prohibition had made it a profitable business. Then they began dealing in chippies. They'd paid him well to look the other way, first with the 'shine, and then with the girls. He even got to sample the wares, so to speak, which sweetened the pot for him. They were not men to cross, and betraying them was not an option for him.

He'd known both Joe and Ray when they were younger, before they got into making 'shine. Joe always had a mean streak, but it was much worse now. Atlee figured too much sampling of his product had burnt any remaining kindness out of him. Ray had always followed his big brother's lead. He still had some decency in him, but that seemed to be waning fast, and he was becoming just a weaker version of Joe.

Putting the men and their activities out of his mind, Atlee stood, grabbed his hat off the peg on the wall, and headed for the door. Time to head home for supper.

Nineteen

A GLIMMER OF PEACE

March 1934

In those dark, quiet moments late at night, when Ruby huddled by the old pot-bellied stove in the hen house, not only did she write about what Joe and Ray did to the girls, but she began to write more and more about herself. Writing about the things that had happened to her was cathartic in a way. Just writing it down helped her to distance herself from it, and she no longer woke in the night from nightmares. Images of Ray forcibly taking her in the middle of the vegetable garden, or Joe cornering her in the basement .... They faded somewhat, like bruises. Still there in her mind, but weaker and less painful. Writing things down seemed to put those things at a distance, and that glimmer of peace grew just a tiny bit.

That first day - they said they were training me and I would be sold and then I asked Ray why and then I fell down the stairs in the main house and

101

broke my leg. It healed funny since Joe refused to get a doctor or do much of anything to help me. He decided I would earn my keep another way. I've been kept here to cook and clean and serve any who want me. I have to lay there and let them do what they want and I die a little each time. I guess it's his bit of revenge because he couldn't make money off me. My revenge will be when I finally get free and tell the world what goes on here.

By accident, Ruby discovered that the combination of writing things down and then burning them was even better. Early one morning, when she'd been writing about her fear of dying if Joe went too far one day, she didn't hear the key in the padlock until it was almost too late. She bent over the stove, dropping the paper in and stirring the coals with the poker. As the paper flared up and quickly turned to ash, she felt almost cleansed. It didn't make a whole lot of sense to her, but she was able to go about her day feeling just a bit lighter in her heart.

Several days later, the first thing Ruby noticed upon waking was the smell of the slop jars. They were getting pretty full, and a bit ripe. If it had still been winter, it would have been fine, but the warmer days of spring meant the hen house was warmer, so the slop jars stank.

Joe and Ray had left four days ago, locking Ruby and the girls in the hen house. Once the snows had melted and the mountain roads were passable, they announced one morning that they were leaving for a couple of days. The girls grabbed what food they could to last a few days, but those supplies were now gone. That was the second thing Ruby noticed – her stomach pinching with hunger.

"I almost hope they come back today. I'm hungry," the younger girl said, echoing Ruby's thoughts.

"I'd settle for emptying the slop jars. That smell is getting' to me," the older girl added.

"At least the pump's not broke and we're got water from the well. Fill up, ladies – that's breakfast." The girls groaned, but they did as Ruby suggested.

Shut in as they'd been for four days, Ruby had shared her practice of writing and burning with the girls. At first, they thought it sounded crazy, but before too long, they were writing in the margins of pages torn from an old magazine. The nightly burning of the pages in the old stove together had become a ritual they all enjoyed.

Several hours later, they heard the sound of a car in the yard. Joe and Ray were back, this time with two more girls. Once sprung from the hen house,

Ruby went to the big house to start cooking a meal. All the while, she knew what the new girls were facing upstairs – rape and 'training'. Once the slop jars were dealt with and the hen house aired out, the girls Ruby considered veterans of the place joined her for some bread and peanut butter.

"Never thought peanut butter would taste so good," the older one said. As a thump sounded upstairs, she looked up at the ceiling. "Isn't there anything we can do for them?"

"Just run them a hot bath later, and offer a hug and sympathy." Ruby shook her head. "Now you know how I've felt every time this has happened."

"God!" was the younger girl's only response.

Twenty

VULTURES GATHERING

There were now four girls at the house, plus Ruby. This puzzled her, as it was not the norm. Usually, the girls stayed for three to four weeks before Joe and Ray sold them on, taking their profit. But this time the two older girls had been there for three months, and the two new girls for two. Ruby couldn't help but wonder what was different this time. She didn't have long to wait to find out.

"You have a week to get everything ready," Joe informed her.

"For what, Sir? What's happening?" she asked hesitantly.

"I'm havin' guests next weekend. Four buyers for the girls. They'll be stayin' the night too. You make sure those bedrooms are spotless, and the girls are ready."

"Kinda strange them comin' here, isn't it, Sir?" she ventured.

"It's none of your damn business," and he shoved her toward the stairs. "Now get on it. I swear, you're slower than molasses in January!" Joe turned to stomp on out of the house.

"And you, girl …." It was Ray, coming out of the living room and stopping in front of her as she stood on the bottom stair. "You better make sure the food is real good. You been slippin' lately."

"Sorry, Sir," she mumbled, not looking at him. "I'll try harder." She dared not look at him, or he'd see the gleam in her eyes.

"Make sure you do. Lotta money ridin' on this weekend. Things better be nigh unto perfect, or you'll regret it." With a laugh, Ray followed Joe out the front door.

A small smile curved Ruby's lips. She watched the door slam behind Ray before she continued up the stairs. *So you noticed my little 'accidents' with the food, did you? Bully for you! I think that means I need to back off for now, though. I'd like nothing better than to poison the whole bunch of you next weekend, but I don't think I'm brave enough for that.*

The next week passed in a blur for Ruby. Since she'd been letting things slide, she had even more to do than usual. Joe wanted to make a good impression on these buyers. While she could care less about that, she figured if they were happy, they'd be nicer to the girls. Or at least that's what she hoped. At this point, it was about all she could do for them. So she cleaned till the house shined, even finding time to bake a blackberry pie with the berries the girls picked. Ruby even tried the recipe she found on the back of a box of the new Ritz crackers – something called a mock-apple pie. She'd have preferred using real apples, but they were getting scarce in the middle of summer.

The first car arrived just before noon on Saturday. There were two men in it, Yankees by the sound of them. Joe ushered them into the living room, and Ruby brought them coffee and some cookies. As per Joe's orders, the four girls were to stay in the hen house until everyone had arrived. He claimed he didn't want anybody to have an advantage.

Another car arrived shortly after the first, and by midafternoon, three of the expected buyers sat in the living room, chowing down on cookies and coffee.

"C'mon, Joe. What're you waiting for? Let's see these girls of yours," one of the Yankees said. "Treat me right, and I might just take more than one off your hands."

107

"Yeah. I'm getting impatient to sample the honey, y'know?" laughed the other one.

"Now gents, we're not all here yet. It'd be rude not to wait a respectable amount of time for Doris to get here."

"Since when you been concerned about bein' rude, Joe? C'mon …."

"Look, buddy, I don't aim to make her mad. I've heard she's got deep pockets, and I aim to have a share of what's in them."

Eavesdropping from the kitchen, Ruby was stunned to think one of the people who was coming to buy girls from Joe, for a brothel, was a woman. That had never occurred to her, and she wondered how a woman could have a hand in taking young women and making whores out of them. It didn't seem possible. It wasn't right.

Just then a horn sounded out front, and Joe could be heard warmly greeting someone. "Doris – Glad you made it. We ain't done business before, but I'm thinkin' you'll be pleased with the merchandise."

"We'll just have to see about that now, won't we? I hope y'all didn't start without me," the woman drawled.

"Of course not, my dear. We been waitin' on you. These here boys wanted to get started without you, but I told 'em no way, we'd wait and be polite."

Ruby had never heard Joe be so ingratiating before, so well … polite. Now more than ever, she wanted to see this woman whom he was trying to impress. She grabbed a mug from the cupboard and the pot off the stove, heading to the living room under the pretext of offering the new arrival a cup of coffee. As she entered the room, she heard the woman reply, "You're right, I would have been right put out if y'all started without me. Fair's fair, after all."

"Coffee, ma'am?" Ruby held out the mug to her.

"Why thank you, honey," the woman replied, turning to face Ruby. "I could use a bit of refreshment after my long drive." Ruby found herself looking at a stunningly beautiful woman, dressed to the nines. Not what she expected.

Ray shooed Ruby out. "Bring the girls over in about half an hour. That should be enough time."

Ruby took the coffee pot back to the kitchen, and then crossed the yard to the hen house. She unlocked the padlock with the key kept over the door, and went inside. Silently, the four girls looked up at her from where they sat on the bunks.

"Ladies, they want me to take you over to the house in a few minutes. I am so sorry! It makes me sick!"

"It's okay, Ruby. We don't blame you," the youngest said softly.

"No, it's not okay, but thanks for sayin' that. Just remember about the farm … if you can get there." That said, the five women clung together, dry-eyed, but gathering strength from each other.

Twenty-One

AN UNEXPECTED PLAN

Ruby ushered the girls into the living room, and then stood off to the side. She watched as the male buyers stood and began to inspect the girls. One of the Yankees seemed to enjoy making the girls uncomfortable, slowly circling each of them, touching their hair, their breasts, their behinds.

Next he'll check their teeth, thought Ruby. *Like he'd buying a horse or a cow — or a slave. But that's how he probably sees it. They're not people to him, they're chattel … tools … things. It makes me so angry!*

"Okay, gentlemen … and lady," Joe inclined his head to Doris. "This how it'll work. You have until supper to get acquainted with the girls. You'll have a second chance after supper for sure. On that little table over there in the corner, there's a box of envelopes and some paper. Each of the girls has a number." He pointed to each of the girls in turn, calling out as he went, "One … Two … Three … Four. If you want to bid on a girl, write your bid on a piece of paper, seal it up, and put the girl's number on the envelope. In the mornin' I'll unseal the envelopes, and the highest bidder wins the girl. We clear?"

"Sure. Seems fair," one said.

"I think I'll get acquainted with this one right now," another said as he dragged one of the girls from the room.

Joe barked at Ruby, "Gimp – supper at 6:00. Now go!"

As Ruby turned to leave, she noticed Doris watching her. It was then that Ruby realized Doris had observed the whole introduction of the girls and the demeaning inspection process, but had not participated. That seemed odd, but then again, who knew what was normal for these sort of people. As the men left with their choice of girls for the afternoon, Ruby noticed that Joe and Ray stayed behind to talk to Doris.

"You didn't try to claim one of the girls. Gotta wonder why?" Ray asked.

"Oh, I'm pretty sure I know 'xactly who I want. You'll just have to wait till mornin' to find out," Doris answered, laughing.

Ruby saw Joe stand and go over to the side table where he kept a few bottles of liquor. "You fancy somethin' stronger than that coffee, darlin'?"

"Too early for me. I like to keep my wits about me. But you go ahead if you feel the need." With that, Doris rose from the couch. "I think I'll just go up to my room and settle in. Ray, will you show me up? I'd hate to walk in on one of the others if I got the wrong room."

Ruby set about putting the chickens in the oven to roast. As she peeled the spuds, a mindless task, she tried hard not to think about what was happening upstairs. Instead, she thought about Doris. Ruby fancied herself able to read people pretty well, but Doris had her puzzled. She didn't look or act like Ruby supposed a madam would, and she found that very puzzling.

Ruby was almost done cleaning up after supper, putting the last of the pans to soak in the sink, when Joe came into the kitchen.

"Gimp – Doris wants to see you. She's in the blue bedroom." He gripped her upper arm and squeezed. "You do whatever she wants, y'hear? I don't care what it is –you just keep her happy. Now git!"

Ruby had no idea what to expect as she limped up the stairs and knocked on the door of the blue room. She'd heard about women who preferred other women for sex. But if that's what Doris wanted, she had no idea what to do. Or how to act. In an odd way, it seemed less immoral than what the men were doing to the girls.

Ruby knocked, and Doris called out, "Come in." She was sitting on the hard chair at the small dressing table, fully dressed.

"You ... you asked to see me, ma'am?" Ruby stammered out.

"That I did. You interest me greatly." Doris paused, patting the end of the bed across from her. "Sit. I'll get a crick in my neck talkin' to you if you keep standin'." As Ruby hesitantly sat on the end of the bed, Doris laughed softly. "Relax, darlin'. I don't bite. Tell me what happened to your leg."

"What?" Ruby asked, puzzled.

"Tell me what happened to your leg," Doris repeated.

"Why?"

"So I'll know if I can trust you. Just tell me."

And so Ruby explained how she'd fallen down the stairs, how Joe and Ray had refused to get help, and how they tried to set her leg, but did a poor job of it.

Doris was silent when Ruby finished, just looking at her. Then she nodded. "I have a question for you. Do you want to leave here? Yes or no?"

"Of course I do. I tried to get away once, but … well, I barely survived the beatin'. It wasn't worth it." Ruby looked at Doris angrily. "Why would you ask me that? It's cruel to give hope and then tromp all over it. I wouldn't think another woman would do that. We should be stickin' together, but what you do …" Ruby realized she was running on at the mouth, in danger of angering this woman whom Joe said she had to please. She rubbed at her forehead. "I'm sorry. I just …."

"Don't be. I know you're sick at heart, and probably real confused as to why I'm askin' you questions. You most likely think I wanted you up here for some naked carryin' on, don't you? While I'll allow as there's some measure of pleasure in that, it's still not what I prefer."

Ruby scrunched up her face in confusion. "Why are you talkin' to me like this? What do you …?"

Doris interrupted her. "Darlin', I heard about you from a girl who came to my house a while back. She told me about you and what you did for the girls. I figured I should look in on you. See if you wanted out."

"Of course, I do! But like I said, I tried that and barely survived."

"Okay then. Here's what we're gonna do. We're gonna make a lot of noise in here, like we're havin' a good ol' time. That'll keep Joe happy. Then tomorrow – well, just follow my lead, okay?"

Ruby studied Doris, looking for a lie, for a trap, but what she saw was genuine concern. "I have no reason to trust you, but … but for some reason I do. I may be dumber than two rocks, but … tell me what to do."

A kernel of hope blossomed in Ruby's chest as Doris whispered her plans to her. Later, they lay side by side on the bed, smothering their giggles with pillows. They had put on quite a show for Joe, if he was listening as they suspected, and fully clothed, they fell asleep on the narrow bed.

Twenty-Two

THE AUCTION

The next morning, Ruby hurried down the stairs to get breakfast started. Joe met her at the bottom of the stairs.

"You have a good time last night?" He leered at her, leaning against the bannister.

Ruby thought for a second, then nodded. "As a matter of fact, I did. Now if you'll let me on by, I'll get started on breakfast."

"Don't you start gettin' uppity with me, Gimp!" Joe shook his fist at her, glaring, and she flinched, expecting a blow. "Them girls be movin' on today, but not you. Come evenin', I'll still own you – you keep that in mind. Get that coffee goin' – they'll be needin' it soon."

Ruby stoked the wood stove, and started a large pot of coffee percolating. Her hands shook as she spooned the grounds into the basket. Deciding she'd wait to start the batter for blueberry pancakes until she heard people stirring, she sat down at the kitchen table, her head in her hands. She felt as if her heart was pounding out of her chest, and her mind kept jumping from one thing to another. Doris's plan was a good one, but they just didn't know how Joe would respond. That's what she feared.

The girls were the first ones to come downstairs, and Ruby made sure they drank their special 'morning-after' tea, before they soaked and scrubbed themselves as clean as they were able. She put an extra scoop of blueberries in the girls' pancakes, and after they'd eaten, they helped her carry platters of bacon and pancakes to the others assembled in the dining room.

"Good mornin', darlin'," Doris called out cheerfully to Ruby as Joe snorted.

Ruby swallowed hard and nodded. "Yes, ma'am," was all she could get out in response.

When everyone had eaten their fill, Joe looked over at his brother. "Ray, you wanna get them envelopes from the livin' room? Y'all have had your fun – now let's do a little business here. Gimp – light a couple of those kerosene lamps so I can see the numbers real good."

Ruby could tell that Joe was enjoying being the center of attention as he drew out the drama of the sealed bids.

"So, we have two bids for Number One," he said, fingering the envelopes. "Get over here, girl. Let's see what these fine folks think you're worth." He tore open the first envelope. "Hmmm … four hundred dollars. Not bad. Let's see if this one's better." He tore open the second envelope. "Ah – better. Five hundred dollars. How does that make you feel, girl – to know that's what you're worth?" he said laughing.

The girl looked him in the eyes and spat at him, jumping back out of range as he swung at her. "At least I'll get away from you," she ground out, sidling behind the man who had just bought her.

"Here, Joe. Here are the bid envelopes for Number Two," interjected Ray, distracting his brother from the girl.

There were three bids for Number Two, and two apiece for Numbers Three and Four. Within half an hour, the auction was done, the four girls sold to their new owners.

"Well, thank y'all. Been a pleasure doin' business with you. Doris, sorry you didn't get anybody." Joe started to stand.

Ray stopped him. "You've got another one here, Joe," and he handed him the envelope.

"What's this now?" Joe was puzzled, looking at the envelope. "Number Five? There were only four girls up for sale."

"But you have five girls here," spoke up Doris. "And I put in a bid for this one here," she added, gesturing at Ruby.

Joe glared at her. "She's not for sale."

"Why ever not? I thought you were in business to make money. Are you rejectin' my bid without even lookin' at it?" Doris shot back.

Joe stood. "She's not for sale," he repeated, tearing the envelope in half.

"Then I'm done here." Doris stood, making a show of pulling on her gloves. "Looks like I wasted my time comin' all the way out here, since you don't want to do business with me. Don't contact me again, Joe. And don't bother to see me out." The sound of the front door slamming behind Doris rang in the awkward silence that followed.

"Okay. Time for us to go, too," said one of the buyers. "Let me get your cash, and I'll be out of your hair." A short time later, the buyers' cars were gone from the yard, and the living room was empty, except for Joe, Ray, and Ruby.

"This your idea, girl? Did you put her up to biddin' on you?" Joe rounded on Ruby.

She took a step back from him. "No, Sir. I didn't do that. No, Sir."

"Get out. You got work to do cleanin' up after that lot. Get on with it," he yelled at her. As she stumbled from the room, Joe spun to face Ray. "You knew there was an extra envelope. Why didn't you just leave it behind? You didn't have to bring it in here."

Ray shrugged. "Thought it was fair. Money's money, after all."

"You knew what was in it, didn't you?"

"No, not for sure. But I figured it was about her. Why did you refuse Doris? You heard her – now she won't ever be doin' business with us."

"The Gimp ain't up for sale."

"But why not? She's been here long enough for sure. Shouldn't she ..." Ray argued.

Joe cut him off. "Doesn't matter. She gave up the chance to leave here when she ran off. She stays!"

"Joe, that makes no sense. I think you just want somebody to do all the work around here so you don't have to."

"Hell, I'd sure rather eat her cookin' than yours," Joe came back.

"But it's not about that, is it? I'm thinkin' you won't sell her 'cause … you want to keep her around so you can punish her for defyin' you." Ray was getting angry.

"So what if I do? It doesn't concern you."

"I think it does! I'm not against keepin' a girl here to do the chores and for us to fuck whenever we want, but what about the money Doris was offerin' for her? You know she has money, and then you just turn her down like that?"

"The subject is closed! The Gimp stays!" yelled Joe.

"And I say she goes! I'm takin' her down to Doris tomorrow mornin'! Hopefully, she'll still buy the girl."

Joe grabbed Ray and spun him around. "No, you ain't!" he screamed, taking a swing at Ray.

A horrified Ruby watched from the kitchen doorway as the two men fought. She saw Joe nail Ray in the gut, doubling him over. But as Ray came up, he fell against the coffee table, sending the lit kerosene lamps crashing to the carpet. The lamps shattered, spraying kerosene across the rug, igniting it in a whoosh. Standing, Ray managed to deliver a solid punch to Joe's chin, connecting hard. Staggering back, Joe tripped over a footstool and fell, his head hitting the stone hearth with a loud thunk. He didn't move again.

"Oh, God – Joe, answer me … Joe?" The only response ray got from his brother was the growing pool of blood beneath Joe's head.

Grabbing the table cloth off the dining room table and limping into the living room, Ruby tried to beat out the flames as they spread. When the table cloth caught fire, she flung it aside. Nothing seemed to help as the spilled kerosene spread the fire to the furniture and drapes, which caught fire easily.

Ray grabbed Ruby's arm as she stood gaping at the flames. "Go on! Get out of here." He jerked his head toward his brother's body. "He's dead. Can't hurt you anymore. And I … just beat it." As Ruby stumbled for the back door, she heard Ray say, "Joe, you always said you'd come to a fiery end. I just didn't figure it'd be like this."

Ruby stopped in the hen house long enough to grab her shawl and walking stick. She had no idea of where she was going to go, but at least it would be away from here. Then she remembered what Doris had told her. "If he won't sell you to me, run off while them boys are hagglin' over the money. I'll be waitin' uphill a bit from where the drive hits the road. I'll wait for a couple of hours."

As Ruby limped across the yard toward the woods, she heard glass breaking, and looked back to see the fire explode the living room windows. Fire and bits of glass rained down on the wooden porch. Just then Ray burst through the front door, clutching the valise into which Joe had been putting the cash from the bids. He leaned against the porch post, coughing, then ran to Joe's car still parked in the yard. Seconds later, that car roared past Ruby and down the rutted drive.

Figuring there was no one to give chase anymore, she limped down the drive, not taking cover in the trees. She looked back once, to see the fire leaping up the side of the old house toward the roof. As she struggled along, she prayed that Doris would be where she said she'd be. If not … well, she'd cross that bridge when she came to it.

Twenty-Three

FREEDOM

Plant the walking stick, stumble on forward. Plant the stick, pull herself along. After the better part of an hour, Ruby wasn't sure which was harder, making her body pull herself down the drive, or making her mind let that happen. She wanted to stop, to simply lay down by the side of the drive and stop trying. But … Joe was dead, Ray was gone, and if she could just make it to the meeting spot, maybe, just maybe, she could …. Ruby didn't even know what she hoped for at this point. There was a part of her, a small part of her that hoped for better things. Plant the stick, stumble forward ….

Ruby made it to where the drive met a bigger road, and turned left, uphill, as Doris had said. She wondered if Doris would actually be there, but she wouldn't be all that surprised if the woman wasn't. It wouldn't matter, she was free and would somehow find her way out. She came around a bend in the road to find Doris leaning against the side of her car.

"You're here. You're really here!" she whispered, limbs trembling as she planted her walking stick. Thunder rumbled close by.

"You made it, darling!" called out Doris, and she rushed forward, folding Ruby in a hug. "Let's get movin' before Joe and Ray catch up to you."

"We don't have to worry about that. They're not comin'. Joe's dead, and Ray drove off like hell on wheels," managed Ruby.

"What do you mean, Joe's dead?"

"They fought. Joe fell and hit his head. They knocked over the kerosene lamps ... there was a fire ... Ray ran off," Ruby stammered out.

"I think you caught a break there. They won't be lookin' for you now." Doris gestured for Ruby to get in the car. Thunder rumbled again as Doris started the car. The skies opened up as the car wound its way down the mountain.

Sheriff Atlee was just finishing a sweep around the outskirts of Dalton, when a car tore past him. "What the hell?" He spat out, recognizing Joe's car with Ray at the wheel. "Where's he goin' in such an all-fired hurry?" Curious now, Atlee flipped on his siren and followed Ray until he pulled over. "Where's the fire, Ray? And where's Joe?" The sheriff leaned on the open car window.

Ray looked straight ahead, hands clutching the steering wheel. "Funny you should ask it like that, Sheriff. Joe's dead. He swung at me. I had to fight back. He fell and hit his head and the lamps got busted and there was fire everywhere." He stopped and took a shuddering breath, finally looking up at Atlee. "I had to defend myself, I did."

"What happened to the girls?"

"Sold off just this mornin'."

"All of 'em? Even the Gimp?"

Ray paused, looking up at Atlee. "Her too. Why you care about her?"

"Don't really. Just makin' sure she won't come back to haunt us."

"Not much chance of that." He glared. "You gonna try and run me in now – for Joe, for the girls, for whatever else you can think of?"

Atlee straightened, looking over the top of the car. "I should, but … I do that, you'll tell about me helpin' you fellas all these years. That'd ruin me, for sure. I think it's time for you to move on, someplace else, and find a new line of work."

"Yeah, I hear Richmond's nice, or maybe Norfolk."

"Just be far from here. We both got reasons to keep our mouths shut about what went on up there."

"Deal, Sheriff. You keep your trap shut, I'll do the same." With that, Ray put the car in gear and sped off.

As Atlee watched Ray disappearing down the road, he decided he'd better head on up to Joe's place and check things out for himself. By the time he got there, the fire was out, doused by the earlier rain storm. He sat in his car for a few minutes, watching what was left of the house smolder, and then drove off. He made plans to return in a few days when the place cooled off. If there was anything left of Joe, he would bury it in the woods, and leave it at that.

After a night spent with a bottle of moonshine and his conscience, the next morning Atlee picked up the phone and placed a call to the sheriff in Roanoke. "Sheriff Carter, remember you askin' me to look for two men named Joe and Ray?"

"Yeah. What did you find?" Carter asked anxiously.

"Did some more diggin', and I'm pretty sure I found 'em, but it's a dead end."

"What d' ya mean?"

"Well, I found a house like what that chippie described, and it did belong to a guy named Joe. But when I went out there, the house was burnt right down to the ground. No sign that anybody'd been livin' there for a while, either."

"So, like you said, a dead end."

"'Fraid so. Can't tell if that's the place the gal you're lookin' for, that … Ruby … was talkin' about. Wish I had better news for you."

"Not your fault it didn't pan out. Thanks for doin' what you could."

After Carter hung up, Sheriff Atlee sat for several long minutes, staring at his desk top, his head in his hands. *Everything is different now. Joe's dead. The deal with Ray will hold as long as Ray never gets it into his head that I'll roll on him. I still regret I didn't get her on a bus before Joe took her back. I hope her new place is better — couldn't be much worse.*

Twenty-Four

AT DORIS'S HOUSE

April 1934
Raleigh, North Carolina

Life at Doris's house was not what Ruby expected. At first glance, the place was a tall, elegant older house on the outskirts of Raleigh, North Carolina. The house was surrounded by a lush green lawn, and a circular driveway led from a quiet street and back again. A wide wrap-around porch with several rocking chairs completed the idyllic picture.

As Doris stopped the car in front of the house and stepped out, a young woman rose from one of the rockers and rushed down the steps to hug Doris warmly.

"*Bonjour, madame*. Welcome home," she said linking arms with Doris. "All is well here, and I can see you were successful." Turning back to Ruby she said, "My name is Celine. Welcome to our home."

Ruby leaned against the side of the car and stared, mouth agape, first at the house, and then at Celine. "It's beautiful, but ... what is this place? I thought ...."

Laughing, Celine interrupted her. "This is our home, as I said." Gesturing for Ruby to follow her, she started for the house, turning back to see Ruby grab her crude walking stick from the car. As Ruby began to limp after her, Celine cried out, "Oh, you poor thing! One more thing we must fix for you, *non*? I find you an elegant cane ... maybe ivory?" Celine continued to chatter as she returned to Ruby, linked arms with her, and led her into the house. Doris followed, grinning at Ruby's expression.

Within a short amount of time, Ruby found herself ensconced in her own room, across the hallway from a well-appointed bathroom. She sat, bemused, as Celine bustled about the room. She wanted to question the girl, but couldn't get a word in edgewise.

"Come, come ..." Celine gestured for Ruby to follow her. "You soak in tub. Relax and let your troubles melt away. I find you clothes and a new stick, *oui*?"

"You're French, right? How did you end up here?" Ruby asked as she followed Celine.

"Oh, my story I will tell you another time. Now is about you." Celine started the water running in the deep tub, adding a handful of dried herbs. At Ruby's curious look she said, "Rosemary mostly ... to relax your mind. Now give to me those clothes, Ruby. I will find you new things and burn these, *oui*?"

Ruby sank into the tub of herb-scented water, a small smile on her lips, despite her uneasiness. *The way she says my name, like there's an 'h' before the 'R', and a little roll to it. Makes it sound sort of exotic. I like that.* After several minutes, she found that she was indeed able to relax, just a bit. Her mind kept trying to wander to her uncertain future, but she reined it in. She would talk to Doris as soon as she could, but for now it was enough to focus on the moment.

When she awoke, Ruby panicked. She could tell it was late in the morning, and her first thought was that Joe would be very angry she hadn't made breakfast. She started to swing her legs over the side of the bed, at first not recognizing her surroundings. Then it all came crashing back. The fire, Joe lying there, Ray driving past her, Doris, Celine, this house ... freedom. Or at least, if she was now property of Doris, it most likely wouldn't be so bad. With that thought. Ruby lay back down, snuggling under the crisp sheets and light blanket, listening to the noises of the house. It was very quiet. A couple of people walked past in the hallway, talking softly. Women by the sound of them. A dove cooed in a tree outside. A dog barked in the distance.

When Ruby woke again, it was afternoon. She dressed quickly with the clothes she found in the closet and dresser, and then went in search of Doris. True to her word, Celine had managed to find her a new walking stick – a carved ivory cane, no less.

"There you are, darlin'. I thought you'd sleep clear through till tomorrow," Doris greeted her when Ruby knocked on the partially open office door.

"I need to know some things," Ruby began.

Doris laughed. "I'll just bet you do. This all must be a bit confusin' to you. So what do you want to know?" She motioned for Ruby to sit in one of the chairs in front of her desk.

"For starters, what is this place? And what am I expected to do here?"

"Ah. Well, for starters," Doris smiled, echoing Ruby, "this is my home. I live here. And sometimes I take in young women who've been treated badly. I give them a place to heal and let them figure out what they want to do next."

"But isn't this a brothel?" asked Ruby abruptly.

133

"Well now, it is, but mostly it's not. None of the young ladies under my care have to do anythin' they don't want to do. Ever. They are never forced, only asked. And they can say no."

"What if they want nothin' to do with that life anymore?" Ruby wasn't sure if she believed Doris, or not.

"Then they have nothin' to do with it. They can earn their keep cookin' or cleanin', if they want to help out. When they're ready, they move on." Doris nodded at Ruby. "I can see it in your face – you want to believe me, but you're findin' it hard to trust me too."

"So what d'you expect me to do? I am never spreadin' my legs for a man again! You can't make me do that." Ruby's voice rose.

"Calm yourself, darlin'! I wouldn't do that to you! You are free to stay here as long as you need to. I know for a fact that you're a good cook, so if you want to help in the kitchen, that'd be right nice of you. Nothin' else you need to do."

"Back on the mountain, you said a girl told you about me. Who was it?"

"Do you remember a girl named 'Rose'?"

Ruby looked thoughtful. "I do. Sweet girl. A little on the chubby side. Could sing like an angel."

"That's her. She was here about six months ago. She told me about you, about what you tried to do for the girls, about how you were treated. I decided I needed to see for myself. I got in touch with some folks I used to do business with, and they helped me get an invite to that miserable auction."

"If you knew about Joe and Ray, why didn't you send the law after them? What they did was so much worse than just runnin' a brothel."

"I'd never heard tell of them before, and I didn't know how bad it was 'til I saw it for myself." Doris paused, shaking her head. "Ruby, I have to tread softly when it comes to the law. Since part of this place is still a brothel, if I talked to the wrong lawman about Joe and Ray, they could shut me down, or worse."

"You mean one of the sheriffs who's not on the up-and-up?"

"The same. I walk a fine line here."

Ruby looked at Doris, thoughtfully. "Why do you do this?"

"Do what?"

"Take in girls like me. Rescue us."

"Because once upon a time, I was not that different from most of the girls here. But I got very lucky. Met a fine man who didn't care about my past. My Eli was a special man. That's his fancy dress cane Celine found for you. We lived in New Orleans, where he had a couple of businesses. We were married for ten years before he died." Doris stood and paced to stand, looking out the window. "His partners, because of my past, thought that they could cheat me out of my share." She turned to grin at Ruby. "They soon learned that this was one woman who wouldn't be cheated. Eli had taught me well, and his partners found out I knew the business as well as they did. I let them buy me out, but they paid dearly for underestimating me."

"But why do this? With the money you could travel or start over somewhere else."

"I do this," she gestured around the room, "because nobody deserves to be treated like you girls were, not even a chippie. When he died, my husband left me with the means to help girls like you, Ruby. I was lucky, you weren't. As sappy as it sounds, I want to make up for that. To return the favor, I guess."

Just then Celine poked her head in the door, "Ah, there you are, *ma chére*. I was wondering where you had got off to," she said to Ruby.

"Celine, would you show Ruby the kitchen? I'm not sure who's cookin' tonight, but maybe they would like a little help. I need to finish these bills before supper. The grocer's seems off a bit," said Doris, returning to the desk and putting on the glasses that had been atop her head.

Twenty-Five

ONCE AGAIN

Over the next few days, Ruby talked to the other girls living at the house. There were six, besides Doris, Celine and now Ruby. And every one of those six backed up what Doris had told her. They were free to go, when they felt ready. They were free to earn some money in the oldest profession, if that was what they chose to do. What they wanted to do with their lives, with their futures, was up to them. Slowly, Ruby came to believe that she too might have a future.

One day, about a week after coming to the house, Ruby took a break from her cooking duties. She had a couple of hours until it would be time to make supper, and she decided to explore the garden behind the house. A pad of paper clutched in her hand, she set out to find a quiet place to begin writing again. The pad, which she had found in a drawer in the house's library, looked to be blank ledger sheets.

As she had learned at Joe's, any paper would do since it would end up as ash anyway.

Ruby knew that to the left of the house was a large kitchen garden that supplied much of the produce for the house. The garden to the right was something of a mystery to her. From the house's second floor windows, Ruby could see pathways lined with flower beds and bushes. There were a few stone benches, and back a little farther, almost to the edge of the woods, was a simple gazebo. That was Ruby's goal as she moved slowly along a pathway of crushed stone. Her new cane made it much easier for her to get around, but she still limped badly and moved slower than she'd like.

Ruby settled gratefully onto a bench in the gazebo. She closed her eyes, savoring the sounds and smells of the garden around her. Bees hummed among the flowers beside the gazebo, and the rich scent of the blossoms on the nearby magnolia tree was almost intoxicating. For several years now, Ruby had carried fear around with her like a heavy woolen coat, weighing her down. Now that she no longer constantly feared for her safety, now that the burden of her fear had been lifted, Ruby was trying to figure out just what it was that she was feeling. Hunching over the pad, she began to write.

I don't know what I thought I was getting into, but Doris's place is not what I expected. Here

139

there's peace and the freedom to choose. I could stay in bed all day if I wanted, and nobody would beat me for it. Doris thinks that I should write to Ma and Pa, that my fears about their reaction don't amount to a hill of beans. Maybe, but I just don't know what ...

Ruby looked up at the sound of steps on the gravel path. Celine waved at her and started to turn back.

"I will not disturb you. I was just going to sit here a while and listen to the garden. It makes my heart lighter."

"Don't go." Ruby patted the bench beside her. "Come sit with me."

"What is it you were writing?" Celine asked, sitting down.

"This? I guess you could call it my journal. I started keeping a journal of a sort at Joe's place. It really was just a stack of mismatched pieces of paper, whatever I could find. I was keepin' a record of what he did to us. One day, I hoped to bring him down with it, but the bastard died and his brother ran before that could happen. And when I escaped, I had to leave it behind."

"It would have felt good to be the one to bring them down, *non*?"

"True, but at least I know they won't be hurtin' anyone else ever again there. That helps.

"And what do you write about now? Surely things here are not so bad for you to write about."

Ruby smiled at the concerned look on Celine's face. "When I wasn't writin' about what Joe and Ray were doin', I would write out my feelings, the pain and anger, the shame I felt. It helped me to stay sane there. It made me feel just a little bit lighter, more whole. And then, every so often, I would throw what I'd written into the fire. Poof – it was gone. Writing my feelings down helped, but seein' it burn up made the bad almost go away. Not quite, but almost."

"Does it not hurt you to remember those things? How can you move on if you are always remembering the past?"

"I'm workin' on that. It takes time. When I write about things, it lightens the load in my heart. I can get rid of a little bit of the anger and pain inside of me. Like when you cut yourself. You bleed, the blood flows out, and then you heal up. Like that."

Celine shook her head. "Sometimes I wonder if I will ever be healed. I have been here for two years now. My body has healed, but my heart … my soul … it is, as you say, not so easy, you know."

"I do know. My leg will always be deformed, my face scarred most likely. There's not much I can do about that. But my heart and soul? That's why I write."

Celine rose from the bench to pace across the gazebo and back, head bent as she thought about what Ruby had said. "Do you think it would work for me? That I could write away some of what is heavy on my heart?"

"I'm bettin' it would. All you can do is try. I probably shouldn't ask, and you can tell me to mind my own business if you want, but what is it that you need to write about? You always seem to be so content and confident."

"If that is how you see me, then I must be a very good actress, like your Katharine Hepburn. Maybe it is time to tell you my story so you will understand what I carry on my heart." Celine sat back down next to Ruby.

"I'd like to hear it."

Celine looked down at her hands clasped tightly in her lap. "It was one week before my eleventh birthday, when my father sold me to one of our neighbors." At Ruby's gasp, she patted her arm. "This was in the old country, in France, but even so, it was not done. Papa lied to the man about my true age. The man gave him a lot of money to marry me, and it was done. We were poor, and Papa had too many mouths to feed, so ... so I was sold off. It would not have been so bad, except that the man was much older than me, and very mean. He enjoyed beating me and forcing himself on me. I do not know how Papa could not have known, but he did nothing to stop it."

"You poor thing – you were just a child." Ruby wrapped an arm around Celine as she continued.

Celine snorted. "Not a child for long. After third time I lose a baby, he started sending his friends to take me, to punish me. Finally, my Papa did something. He went to the authorities, but it was too late. My husband somehow found out, and we fled to this country. Things did not change much after we settled in New Orleans, except that now he made money off me, off my body. I had been his property for almost ten years, when one night, a business partner accused him of cheating and shot him dead. I ran, and it was almost a year later that Doris found me." Celine smiled at the memory. "Actually, I found her – I tried to steal her purse and she would not let it go."

"Your Papa should be ashamed! That he would sell his own little girl ...."

"I imagine he was, but … well, I have come to understand that what he was doing … it was what he thought he had to do so they all did not starve."

"You sound like you have forgiven him. How could you do that?"

"Ruby, I was betrayed not once, but two times, by men who were supposed to protect me, first, by my Papa and then, by my husband. I don't know if I can ever forgive them for that. But I know I have to try. Never forget, no, that I cannot do. But I must forgive. I am not there yet. Maybe this thing you do with the writing, it will help me."

"I think it will help us both. Let's go see if we can find you a notebook of some kind to use." Ruby stood, linking her arm through Celine's and drawing her off toward the house.

It soon became a common sight, Ruby and Celine hunched over pads of paper, scribbling away. The other girls became curious, then joined in. The idea that their pain and anger would start to flow out of them like the ink out of the pen must have sounded a bit crazy, but one by one they asked Doris for notebooks and began writing.

Ruby began her journal all over again, writing down what had happened to her. As she wrote, she could feel the anger boiling inside of her. She thought about what Celine had said, about trying to forgive, and she wondered if she would ever be able to get to that point. Writing things down lessened the pain and anger, and it made her heart feel a bit lighter, but forgiveness seemed a long way off.

I met Ray on the bus out of Norfolk. He seemed nice, and we talked about the books we'd read. Once we got to Roanoke, his brother, Joe, met up with us. They drugged me and took me to a house …

Another time she wrote:

Men would come to the house from time to time. Joe always wanted me to cook a fine dinner for them. If I hadn't been such a coward, I'd have added poison to it like Tilda tried to do, and I'd have cheered when they all choked and died. They deserved it after what they did — the beatings and the rapes. But I couldn't do it, and they ate my fine dinners, and that was that. Joe would sometimes give me to one of the men. I had no say in the matter. Pain. Shame. I wished I could have killed myself, but the old faith says that's a worse sin than killing someone else. And I couldn't give up that tiny bit of hope that I would somehow get away from that hell.

Once a week, after supper was over and the washing up was done, any of the girls who wanted to would gather in the library where Ruby'd build a fire in the fireplace. One after another, they would tear the pages out of their notebooks and fling them into the fire. Sometimes there were tears, but usually they felt joy at seeing their pages go up in smoke. As Ruby began to burn some of her pages, once again she came to feel something akin to healing in her heart. She doubted she could ever forgive Joe and Ray for what they'd done, but she'd take what she could get, for now.

> *They made me help them. I had to get places ready for the girls. And then I had to clean them up after the men were done with them, and get them ready for another round of 'training'. When I refused, Joe beat me. Said it was a lesson for the girls — don't defy him or you'll get beat up. It near broke my heart. The girls screamed and cried so — all I could do was hug them and cry too.*

It wasn't long before Ruby's journal began to reflect the changes she felt inside. Fear slid away, replaced by the joy of freedom.

> *I took another bath today, a long soak in the tub, with rose petals floating on the water. It felt almost decadent, but smelled glorious. Such joy to be able to be clean again whenever I want.*

I walked down to the end of the long drive yesterday. I just stood there, savoring the fact that I could keep on walking if I wanted. I wasn't locked up anymore. I was free to choose if I stayed or not. I thought my heart would burst.

It was like a stone rolling down a hillside. The more Ruby wrote, the easier it became to write about those awful days. The more she wrote, the better she felt, about herself, about everything that had happened. Not good maybe, but better.

Twenty-Six

THE OTHER SIDE OF THE HOUSE

While Doris's house was a refuge, it greatly confused Ruby that Doris would run a brothel within that refuge. One morning, she met Doris as the woman was closing the door to the west wing of the house.

"I don't understand how you can be involved in all that," Ruby said, waving her hand dismissingly at the door behind Doris.

"Come, let me show you," and Doris turned back to unlock the door.

"What? No! I'm not goin' in there!"

"Silly girl, there's nobody in there right now. I just want you to see this part of the house before you condemn me out of hand. Come along … follow me." Doris opened the door, and Ruby slowly followed her along a short hallway, into a beautifully appointed sitting room. There were several comfortable-looking settees and large chairs, all upholstered in luxurious fabrics. Everything in the room was tastefully done.

"I'll give you it's pretty, but dressin' up a pig … it's still a pig."

"Ruby, that's true. Oh, sit a spell and let's talk this out." Doris settled into one of the chairs, as Ruby perched on the edge of a settee. "Do you remember when you first came here and we talked? And I told you that some of the young women who live here choose to make some money as prostitutes? That was all true – but the important word here is 'choose'. I never pressure any of them, never force them into it. That was done to them before they came to me, and I'll not add to that."

"And I told you I'd never be a part of that world again – I'd rather starve."

Doris nodded. "And I respect your decision. I'll never pressure you to change your mind. But I want you to try to understand why this wing of the house exists." She paused. "How much money do you think it takes to care for a handful of women for a month? Clothes, food, coal – the lot?"

"I never thought about it. I guess … I guess it's not cheap."

"No, no it's not. Like I told you before, I have some money from my late husband, but not enough to keep this house going for long. This may be the 1930s, but women still don't have that many ways to earn money. Can you see me as a schoolteacher or a maid?" Doris laughed as Ruby shook her head. "So, I had to fall back on what I knew, and I knew that the business of pleasure was profitable. This wing of the house brings in enough money to keep us going. The girls keep two-thirds of whatever they make, and they give me one-third. In turn, I only allow a few men to come here, ones who I know will not mistreat the girls. And I give them an elegant setting." She gestured around the sitting room.

Ruby glanced around herself and then down at her hands clasped tightly in her lap. "Okay, I guess I understand what you're sayin'. It just seems kinda wrong that this is what you'd choose to do."

"And there's that beautiful word again – 'choose'. I choose to do this, so that I can help you and the other girls have brighter futures."

"What if you chose to do somethin' else to bring in money? Somethin' legal and all."

"I'd like that, but until that opportunity presents itself, this is what I will continue to do. Let me show you the rest of this wing. If we hurry, we just have time before lunch." Doris stood and reached out a hand to Ruby.

"Doris … I'm not sure if I said it before, but … thank you for takin' me in and tryin' to help me. I don't mean to seem like I'm criticizin' you. I guess my head's still all muddled up."

Doris pulled Ruby up and hugged her. "It's fine, truly. You keep that sharp mind of yours askin' questions, and you keep workin' to put the last few years behind you. You'll get there."

The rest of the wing consisted of two bedrooms, both elegantly appointed, bright with sunlight and smelling of herbs and flowers. Despite her misgivings, Ruby was impressed.

Twenty-Seven

WRITE, BURN, REPEAT

"Ouch!' Ruby tugged a comb through her thick hair. It had grown much longer over the past few years, and she usually contained her mass of auburn hair in a braid down her back. Haircuts had not been possible while she was held captive. Finger waves and pin curls were also things of the past, now seeming too frivolous for her taste.

As she sat combing out her hair in front of the mirror, her eyes fell on the scar across her right cheek, where Joe's ring had cut her. As she touched the scar, she remembered that day and shuddered. But she also remembered something else. Once, when she was little, her mother had put something on a bad scar on her hand, left over from a cut she'd gotten from some rusty wire. The scar was hardly noticeable anymore, and Ruby wondered if maybe she could do the same thing to the scar on her cheek. She fell asleep that night, mulling over what her mother had done.

In the morning, she dressed quickly, and went downstairs to the kitchen. There she found a small jelly jar with a lid. She remembered that her mother had used honey as a base for just about all of her home remedies, and when she looked at the faded scar on her hand, she'd have sworn she smelled lemon. Adding the juice of a lemon to the honey in the jar, she mixed until it looked about right to her.

"Good morning, Ruby," Celine called out, coming through the kitchen door. "I did not know it was your morning to cook."

"I'm on tomorrow. I was just mixing up a potion my Ma used to make."

"For what? It smells good, no matter."

"If I remember rightly, this may help fade the scar here."

As Ruby touched her cheek, Celine smiled. "Of course. Why did I not think of that sooner? It is an old cure, but it works. I am glad to see you taking interest in your looks. You are a pretty *mademoiselle*, no matter what." As Ruby started to protest, she continued, "Now shoo. I have food to make, and you know I must think hard about that."

Ruby laughed. "Do you want me to stay and help you? Cookin' is not your favorite thing."

153

"But of course I want you to stay and help. I was afraid you would not ask."

There followed much laughter and good-natured ribbing as the two young women set about making breakfast for the household.

Celine's notebook was getting pretty full, a fact Ruby commented on one day while they sat writing in the gazebo. "I see you throw some papers into the fire and burn them and send them away. But what's all that you're keepin'? What can't you let go?"

"The pages I throw into the fire ... they're about my Papa, mostly. How he sold me off and did not try to save me. That is what I am able to let go.

"So what're you keepin' in your notebook?"

"Mostly ... mostly it is about the vile husband. About what he did to me. About how his friends enjoyed humiliating me. I cannot seem to make myself throw all that into the fire. I still have much hate inside me, and burning it ... I guess I am not ready to let it go yet."

Ruby nodded and shrugged. "It's not easy, that's for sure. When I write about Joe, about what he did to me, I get boilin' mad all over again. I thought

I'd be done with him by now, but the anger is still there. It's not as strong as it was, but it's still there."

"But how do we get this anger inside to go away?"

"Maybe it won't ever go away completely. So we do what we can. We write it again. And burn it again. Write. Burn. Write. Burn. Again and again and again. Until finally, we feel something change inside."

"And forgiveness? It is almost too much to ask of us, is it not? It will take much writing and burning to get me to forgiving the vile husband." Celine grimaced. "Have you come to forgive Joe and Ray yet?"

"Forgive them? No way will I do that! They deserve to rot in hell for what they did."

"That is most certainly true. We will never forget what we suffered, and maybe forgiveness will never come. But at least a measure of peace maybe we can have."

That evening, when the girls gathered by the fireplace, Ruby watched Celine out of the corner of her eye. Finally, after all the other girls had their turns, Celine stood, threw her entire notebook into the fire, and sat back down. Ruby smiled at her, and handed

Celine a new notebook from the pile on the desk nearby. "Again, my friend, again," she said softly.

Twenty-Eight

A FACE FROM THE PAST

Ruby was in the kitchen, getting a meatloaf ready to go in the oven, when she heard honking from the front yard. Doris was back. She had been gone for three days, and Ruby figured she might be bringing in a new girl. She rinsed off her hands, drying them on her apron as she headed to the front door. Celine, bounding down the stairs, met her there.

"So exciting, it is not? Let us go see how we can help." By the time the girls made it to the porch, Doris was already there, accompanied by a slim, dark-haired girl.

"We have a new guest, Celine. Meet ..."

"Agnes?" interrupted Ruby. "Agnes, is it really you?"

Startled, the girl looked up at Ruby, then her face broke into a huge grin. "Ruby? Saints be praised! I never thought to see you again." Agnes grabbed

Ruby and hugged her tightly. "How did you get away from Joe? No, let me guess," she said as Ruby started to speak. "Doris bought you, right?"

"Not exactly. It's a long story that can wait till you're settled. What happened here?" She gently touched the purple bruise on the side of Agnes's face.

"The usual. Another long sad story."

"Well, when you want to talk, I'll be here. Right now, I've got a meatloaf demandin' my attention in the kitchen."

As Celine led Agnes off into the house, Doris stopped Ruby. "One of your girls, I gather?"

Ruby nodded. "Yeah. One of mine. Joe took a shine to her and kept her around longer than most. I tried to do my best by her. I'm right glad she has a chance now. Thank you for that."

"My pleasure, darlin'. Don't suppose you got any coffee perked up in that kitchen?"

"Sure. My pleasure," Ruby laughed, nodding her head and echoing Doris.

Agnes hugged Ruby. "I was real surprised to see you here, Ruby. I figured, one day, Joe would go too far and kill you, he was that mean."

"Agnes, I got pretty good at stayin' out of his way. And when I couldn't …" Ruby shrugged, "well … at least I'm still around."

It was the girls' turn to sweep and dust the west wing, and they chatted as they worked. Taking a break, Agnes flung herself into one of the large sitting room chairs, dropping her feather duster on the floor. "You remember Della?'

"Sure. She was good people. You seen her?"

"She was in the same house as me for a while, down by Greensboro. She made it out too – just snuck off one day. Last thing she said to me was that she was gonna head up toward Roanoke and try to find your folks' place."

"I hope she made it. I know they'd take her in and help her, despite …"

"Despite what we became, you mean?"

"I guess. My Ma wouldn't hold it against her. And my Pa – he'll follow Ma's lead."

"Why are you still here then? Why haven't you gone home if you're so sure they'd welcome you?"

"I … I guess I'm not ready to see them. I'm still afraid of what I will see in their eyes when they open that door and I'm standin' there."

"Ruby, if they'd take in Della like you said, surely they'd take you in. You're their daughter, after all."

"Oh, I know they'd take me in. It's just ... my Pa had such high hopes for me. I can't help but feel he'd be sorely disappointed in me, that I'm not his innocent little girl anymore."

"Maybe. But if he loves you, he'd come around. You just gotta give him time. What about your Ma?"

Ruby laughed. "She'd hug me tight and not let go. We'd have a good cry, and then she'd dose me with one of her tonics, even if it ain't spring yet. Then ... she'd most likely cry some more, send Pa out huntin', and set me to kneadin' up some bread."

"Practical woman. I like her already. You need to go see her."

"I'm workin' on it. Still got some anger to work out, but I'm getting' there. What about you, Agnes?"

"I'm considerin' my choices. I don't much like myself these days, and I got no family to go home to like you do, so ..." She gestured around the sitting room. "You ever think about comin to work over here?"

"No way! Not me. I just couldn't do that."

"Would you think me awful if I said I was considerin' it?"

"Of course not! Agnes, you're not awful, and you're not a bad person. I can't understand why you'd want to be a … a chippie, after what you've been through. But it's your life, your choice."

"This place is a thousand times better than where I was. Shoot, Joe's was better than where I last was, if you can believe it. I don't feel fit to be 'round decent folk anymore. I wasn't a teacher or a nurse or much of anything before. Sure, I can type a bit, but that's about it. This just might suit me, for now at least."

"You think careful about what you wanna do. If this is it, then okay. But remember – you can always go to my folks' farm and they'll help you sort it out."

"I'll remember that. Enough lollygagging. We'd better get finished here."

Twenty-Nine

DR. FRANKS

May 1934
Raleigh, North Carolina

When the girls locked the door to the west wing behind them, Doris greeted them. "There you are, Ruby. I've been lookin' for you. You've got a visitor," and she motioned for Ruby to follow her into the library.

"Who would want to see me? I don't know anybody hereabouts."

"Patience, darlin'." Doris looked back at Ruby. "I should have said somethin', but I didn't want to get your hopes up." As Doris closed the library door behind them, an older man stood from the chair where he'd been sitting.

"Good afternoon, Ruby. I'm Dr. Franks."

"Afternoon, sir. I'm not sure why a doctor'd want to see me. I'm not sick."

"True, but Doris came to me and told me about your leg. She asked me if there was anything that could be done to help you walk better."

"Dr. Franks, it's mighty nice of you to come out here, but as you can see, my leg is a mess. It's twisted some, and without this cane Celine found for me, I'm not sure … well, I get by okay. I'm not sure what you could do to fix it, anyway."

"Why don't you let me have a look, and I'll be the judge of whether I can help you or not. Come, lie down on the couch here." He smiled at her hesitation. "Don't worry. Doris will be here the whole time. And I promise to be gentle. How 'bout you tell me how this leg got broken."

"What do you want to know?" Ruby asked as she lay down on the couch.

"Oh, dear. Just start at the beginning."

After about a half an hour of Dr. Franks touching her leg, feeling the old break, Ruby was beginning to get almost amused. After her short explanation, he asked her question after question about what had happened, and what had been done to set the leg. What amused her was his demeanor. It was as if he had been presented with a difficult problem, and his mind became focused on finding a

163

solution to that problem. Finally he sat back in the wingback chair, fingers steepled in front of his chest, and stared into space.

Ruby sat up, straightening her skirt. "May I get up now, Dr. Franks?"

"What? Oh, yes. That would be fine."

"So what do you think?" Doris asked coming to sit beside Ruby.

"Well, that all depends on Ruby. The initial break was bad enough, but because the leg was re-injured when she was beaten, I don't think it is possible to ever get it completely back to normal. And I will need to take an X-ray to make sure, but, yes, I do think I can make it better." He leaned forward and took Ruby's hands in his. "Ruby, what I propose to do will not be a picnic. Even with our modern drugs, it will hurt. I'll have to operate on the leg to clean out the debris, and then patch the bones back together, probably with a metal piece. And then it will take close to nine months, start to finish, until you can walk without help. What do you think?"

"I'm not sure what to think. Lord knows, I appreciate your comin' out here and givin' me hope that I could walk some better. But I got no money to pay you. And I'm not about to lay with you just so I can walk better." Ruby jerked her hands back.

"Ruby!" Doris was shocked. "That's rude!"

Dr. Franks laughed. "No, Doris, it's okay. I'm not offended. Ruby, I would never ask that of you. I know you have been through a lot, and as a physician, hell, even as just a man who tries to do good, I would never do anything to hurt you." He stood, walked to a side table, and poured himself a whiskey.

"I'm sorry for jumpin' to conclusions, sir. Sometimes my mouth gets ahead of my brain, I guess."

"It happens to all of us." Dr. Franks sat back down. "Doris is one of my dearest friends; we've known each other longer than either of us will admit. When she came to me about you, I was intrigued. Now that I have seen you – well, I want a chance to try to fix your leg. I can't promise great results, but I'm willin' to try it, if you are. My services would cost you nothing, though I do hear you make a mean meatloaf."

Ruby sat thinking, looking at her damaged leg. Finally, she straightened and stood. "Meatloaf day is this Thursday. I'll set a place for you. After that, you're welcome to try to solve this problem you find so intriguing." She limped toward the door, turning back as she reached it. "Thank you," she said softly as she left.

Thirty

DID IT WORK?

The first thing Ruby was aware of was the pain. It felt like a wall of flame, with the addition of hot pokers jabbing at her leg. She moaned and tried to shift away from the pain, but found she couldn't move.

"More morphine over here, Nurse," she heard Dr. Franks call out. A prick in her arm, and she felt a wave of coolness dousing the pain. She sank back into the healing grasp of sleep.

When Ruby woke the next time, she managed to get her eyes open briefly before someone noticed, and she was given another shot for the pain.

When Ruby woke up the third time, she was much more aware. The pain in her leg was a distant throbbing, and her head felt less like it was stuffed with cotton batting. She lay still, and listened to the noises around her. In truth, there wasn't much to hear. A couple of people talking softly not too far away, the hum and clicking of the ceiling fan, but that was about it. She shifted her weight as best she could in the hard bed, and heard one of the voices abruptly stop speaking. Soon, she heard the sound of crepe soled shoes and the crisp swish of a nurse's uniform.

"Welcome back, Miz Ruby." A kindly face appeared over her. "Now don't you go movin' around much. Dr. Franks wants you to lie as still as you can."

"So thirsty," Ruby managed to croak out.

"I'll just bet you are. Here, let me crank up the head of your bed a bit, and I'll get some ice chips for you to suck on."

Once Ruby was propped up in bed a bit, the nurse spooned a few ice chips into Ruby's mouth. The melting ice soothed her throat, and the coldness acted as a bit of a shock to help clear some of the fog from her mind. Deciding Ruby was awake enough, the nurse handed her the small bowl with ice chips in it. Ruby felt clumsy, like her hands were too big for the rest of her, and holding the bowl took concentration.

"Did it work? Is my leg gonna be better?" Ruby asked around the ice melting in her mouth.

"I'll let Dr. Franks tell you all about it. We've sent to let him know you're awake again. He'll be here shortly." The nurse patted her arm. "I don't know

167

exactly what he did to your leg, but I can tell you he was whistling when he left here."

"That's good, right?"

"I would think so. Now you just go back to sleep till the doctor gets here."

"I don't want to sleep and miss him. I need to know if it was worth it."

"Don't worry, darlin'. I promise to wake you when he comes." With that promise, Ruby allowed herself to sink back into sleep.

"Ruby?" Someone patted her arm. "Ruby? I need to examine your leg. Can you wake up for me?" she heard Dr. Franks say.

"I'm awake. I'm awake," she assured him groggily. "Did it work? Is my leg better?"

He laughed. "Let me take a look, and then we'll talk." He gently unwrapped the splint around her leg, and examined the incision. As soon as he was satisfied, he replaced the splint and rewrapped it.

"Well?" she asked impatiently.

"It's looking good! Incisions are healin' nicely – no infection. Let me explain what I had to do. It was like I thought. Because of the way your leg was broken and not set properly, the ends of the bones had grown calcium deposits. Had to go in and scrape that away. Then I mended the break with a metal plate and some screws. In a week or so, I'll put a proper plaster of paris cast on it."

"Is that why it feels like a throbbin' fire?"

"You're not the first to describe it that way. But yes, that's why. When I leave, I'm goin' to ask the nurses to get some ice packs for around your leg. That'll help keep swellin' down, and put out some of that fire you're feelin'."

"How long till we know if the operation worked?"

"Well … that depends. Since there was only one break, probably six weeks until you can put a little pressure on it."

"That long? I don't know if I can stand not knowin' that long."

"Young lady, considerin' what all you've put up with over the last couple of years, six weeks is nothin'. After that, comes three months on crutches. You'll be able to put some weight on it, but not much."

"Another three months?" she squeaked in dismay.

"Yup. Then we can take the cast off, and shortly after that, you'll start another three months of therapy. You've got to remember, the muscles in that leg haven't been used right in a while, so you're gonna have to teach them what to do again."

"I guess."

"What you got to do now is sleep a lot – that helps with healin', in my experience. Rest up, and let others take care of you for a change. You hungry?"

Her stomach grumbled, and she laughed. "I guess I could eat a bite."

"Figured as much. We've kept you asleep for two days now, so you have some eatin' to catch up on. I'll have the nurses get you some supper. Then it's back to sleep for you. And don't be afraid to ask for something for the pain. Hurtin' just slows down the healin'."

After Dr. Franks left, Ruby ate the simple supper the nurses gave her. She leaned back in the bed, and found herself, for the first time in a long while, praying. *Please God, let it work. Please God, let it work.* She drifted off, silently praying.

Thirty-One

AN OLD FRIEND

A happy squeal from someone at the nurses' station outside her room woke Ruby. "Why you're a sight for sore eyes, young man. Where you been?"

"Miss Lorna, Dr. Franks has me studyin' for the medical boards. That's comin' up in a couple of weeks." Ruby thought the voice sounded familiar, but then she figured she was just groggy with sleep.

"Well, I know you'll do just fine. You listen to Dr. Franks and keep on studyin'. I wanna be able to say one of my orderlies is now a real doctor!"

"I'll try to do you proud. I couldn't take any more of the books today. What you got for me that needs doin'?"

Ruby gasped. She knew that voice. It had been close to five years, but she remembered everything about the young man it belonged to. Once they had been sweet on each other, but they went their separate ways after high school.

He can't see me like this. He'll want to know what all happened to me since we last saw each other. No way can I tell him. … Lordy, please let me be wrong and it's not him.

"Why first off, you can help the young lady in 101 get into her wheelchair. Doc wants her to sit outside for a while today. Then you can do a bed pan run on the men's ward."

"Okay, Miss Gracie. I'm on it."

Ruby tried to roll over and feign sleep, but the splint on her leg prevented that. She knew she didn't have much chance that the earth would open up and swallow her whole, so she had to settle for closing her eyes and trying to breathe slowly.

A cheerful voice called out from the doorway, "Morning, Miss. Your chariot awaits." Ruby heard steps as he neared the bed. Then a gasp. "Sweet Jesus! Ruby? I don't believe this. What …? How did you get …?" He stammered to a halt.

With a sigh, Ruby opened her eyes and looked up at him. "Mornin', Jake Boone. Fancy meetin' you here."

Once Jake had Ruby settled outside in the hospital's garden, he pulled up a chair and sat down next to her. "I can't stay long – Nurse Lorna has me on bedpan duty – but I can manage a few minutes for now. So tell me, how did you end up here?"

"It's a long story. The short of it is that I fell down some stairs, the leg wasn't set right, and Dr. Franks is tryin' to fix it some."

"He's a swell doctor, Ruby. You're lucky to have him."

"That's what I figure, too. So what are you doin' here? Last I saw you was, what … four … no closer to five, years ago. You were in Roanoke, workin' in your family's drug store."

"Yeah. After college, I helped out there as a pharmacist until business got real slow, and then I came down here to Raleigh lookin' for work. Ended up in this hospital, met Dr. Franks, and the rest, as they say, is history. All of which I'll have to tell you later." Jake stood to leave, squeezing her shoulder. "Bed pans await."

"Charming. Have fun." She forced out a laugh. Once she was alone, Ruby tried to relax in the warm sun, but her mind was full of disjointed thoughts. *Did he notice how I flinched when he touched my shoulder? Will he wonder why? Is he gonna let my folks know where I am? Does he even know I'm missing?*

Ruby sat in the sun-filled garden, watching a butterfly fluttering between the flowering bushes, remembering her childhood, remembering Jake. They had met in the small school just outside of Roanoke. At first, he ignored her, seeing as how she was just a girl. But then came the fateful dodge ball game when she proved her worth by winning the game for their team. For several years after that, they had hung around together. Ruby and Jake, along with Fred and Eddie, had gone fishing together, caught frogs, and explored the world. That is, when they weren't all working on their families' farms – except Jake, who helped in his father's drug store.

Ruby smiled, remembering their first kiss. They'd been about sixteen by then, and finally figured out that the fact he was a boy and she was a girl was a good thing. Coming back from fishing one day, after Fred and Eddie had gone their ways, Jake stopped her on the path near her house. He leaned over and gave her a quick peck on the cheek. When he turned to go, she spun him back and gave him a proper kiss. She could still remember his stunned look, just before he took off running.

They'd been sweethearts for a couple of years after that, until she left to go to teachers' college. Then, they just drifted apart. Letters came less and

174

less often, and then stopped. They'd still been fond of each other, but not involved in each other's lives anymore. *It feels good thinking back on those days. Life was good, and we had our futures spreading out in front of us, seemed like. I wonder if I'll ever feel like that again.*

"Miz Ruby? You ready to come on in for some lunch now?" Ruby jerked awake, realizing she had been lost in her thoughts and must have drifted off. George, the orderly she was used to seeing, stood next to her chair.

"Where's Jake?"

"Oh, don't you worry none. Dr. Franks done caught up with him and set him to studyin' again," George replied, smiling, as he started pushing her wheelchair back into the building.

"What's he studyin' for?"

"Why, our Mister Jake's gonna be a doctor, Miz Ruby. He just has to take some big test to prove he's smart, and then he's a doctor."

Ruby was stunned. "That's wonderful, George. When's the test?"

"Couple of weeks, I guess. Here you be, back in your room just in time for Jello and egg salad."

"Could be worse."

"Sure 'nuff – could be no Jello!"

Ruby waited on pins and needles the rest of the day, hoping Jake would come back, and praying that he wouldn't. She dreaded their conversation, not sure what, if anything, she'd reveal about the last few years of her life. She fell asleep that night, troubled, having come to no decision.

Thirty-Two

HE KNOWS

When Dr. Franks came in to check on Ruby the next morning, she was full of questions. "Where's Jake? Do you think he will pass the big test George told me about and become a real doctor? Is he any good? How long have you known him?"

"And a good morning to you too, Ruby." He laughed. "Why all these questions about Jake?"

"We grew up together, Doc. Back in Roanoke. I haven't seen him in years, though."

"Oh, dear. I didn't know he knew you. Is that awkward for you, seeing him now?" Dr. Franks gave her a concerned look.

"I don't know. He only stayed for a few minutes before he had to go. I'm not sure what to tell him next time I see him. Since he works here, he might have seen my records. He might already know what happened to me. He didn't act like it, but ...."

177

"How do you think he'd act if he knew?"

"I'd be afraid he'd treat me like I was dirty, like I wasn't fit to be his friend anymore. I wouldn't exactly blame him if he felt like that, but it'd hurt still. People look down on a woman who's done what I did, even if it wasn't by choice."

"Some do, but ..."

Ruby interrupted him. "Worse would be if he treated me with pity. I couldn't stand that, not from him."

"Ruby, I know for a fact he's not seen your medical records. As an orderly here, he wouldn't be allowed to see them. But ... he's also my protégé, my student. And as such ... Ruby, I'm sorry, but I did discuss your case with him. Anonymously, no names. I imagine he was as shocked to see you as you were to see him. I am so sorry if this makes it awkward for you."

"Awkward?" Ruby managed to squeak out. "So, you're tellin' me he knows all about what happened to me?"

"I only told Jake the bare medical facts. He knows about the fall and your broken leg. He knows that you suffered physical abuse later that made it worse. He doesn't know what you went through emotionally, or what it did to you in here," he thumped his chest. "I didn't give him any details of the abuse. That's for you to tell him, if you choose."

"Is he comin' in here today?"

"Tomorrow. Today he's reviewing chemistry. The medical board is next week, and every bit of studying is important."

"Well, I guess that gives me time to figure out what to say to him."

"Yours just seemed like a perfect teaching case. I wanted to see what he'd make of it, to see what his medical opinion would be. I'm sorry if my doing that put you in a difficult position. Had I known you two knew each other ...." Dr. Franks shook his head.

"It's okay, Doc. If I'm eventually gonna go home, I guess I'd better get used to bein' treated differently. I'm not the same person I was, and .... Besides, maybe talkin' to Jake will help me shake free of what happened."

Thirty-Three

THE STORY TOLD

When Jake got to the hospital the next morning, he had a message to report to Dr. Franks.

"Mornin', Jake. Come on in." Dr. Franks motioned for Jake to enter his office. "Have a seat."

"Am I in trouble, sir?"

Dr. Franks laughed at the look on Jake's face. "Not that I know of. I just wanted to catch you before you saw Ruby."

"Ah. It sure was a shock seeing her the other day."

"I'm sure it was. Jake, if I'd known you two knew each other, I'd never have discussed her case with you."

"I know. It seemed all cut and dried, so clinical, a crippled-up leg, all the physical abuse a nameless patient endured. And then to find out that nameless patient was Ruby? I still don't know how to deal with that."

"How close were you two?"

"We spent lots of time together growin' up. First kiss. Sweethearts for a while. Then college got in the way, and we kinda drifted apart."

"Well, Ruby needs you to be her friend again. If she wants to talk to you about the things that happened to her, just listen with an open mind. Your friend was badly treated. She sees herself as flawed, and she needs your acceptance, now more than ever." Dr. Franks raised a hand as Jake started to speak. "And if she doesn't choose to talk, just be her friend and give her time."

"I know you're right, but honestly, I'm scared to death to talk to her. I don't know if I can be the friend she needs." Jake shrugged. "The Ruby I knew is gone, and I don't know this new Ruby."

"So get on out there and meet this new Ruby. Be her friend. That, and a few prayers wouldn't hurt. Now get. I have reports to finish and patients to see."

Jake found Ruby in the hospital garden. In a wheelchair, with her leg up, she sat in a patch of sun, eyes closed, with a small smile on her lips. He leaned against the doorjamb, just watching her. She looked so peaceful, he hated to disturb her. He figured, after what she'd been through, she deserved a little peace.

Gathering himself, Jake strode up to her chair. "Mornin', Ruby. How you feelin'?"

"Pretty good, Jake, pretty good. How's the studyin' goin'?"

"At this point, it's mostly review, but chemistry was real hard for me. At least I didn't blow up somethin' in the lab like one of my classmates did." He grinned and shook his head.

"You're kiddin' me."

"Nope! Don't know what he did wrong, but it was a mess, for sure. And the professor … his face turned so red I thought he was gonna have a stroke over it."

Ruby laughed, picturing the incident. "Must've been a sight, for sure." Sobering, she looked down at her lap. "Jake, I'm hopin' you can sit a spell with me. We should talk. I figure there's things you need to know."

He grabbed a nearby chair, bringing it over next to her, and sat. "So, what's up?"

Unable to look at him, she studied her hands clasped tightly in her lap. "I know Dr. Franks talked to you about some of the things that happened to me. Were you ever going to tell me that you know?"

"He did discuss it with me, but as a medical case. Everything he told me was about a nameless patient with a badly healed broken leg. Said there'd been some physical abuse which complicated things. That's all. I swear, if I'd known the patient we talked about was you, I'd have been in your room sooner! You gotta believe me, Ruby."

"I do ... it's just I feel I owe you the truth about what happened to me, but I'd hate it if you turned away from me, if you pitied me, or thought I wasn't fit to be around anymore."

Jake pulled in a long, steadying breath, closing his eyes briefly. "First of all, I'm not most people. I figure you're more than fit to be around. We were close once, and I hope you still think of me as a friend. And second of all, you're about the last person I'd pity. You have more strength in you than anybody I know. I have a lot of respect for you, and I'm not about to turn away from you."

"Well, you should."

Jake was quiet for a few moments, just looking at her. "You're tryin' to push me away, aren't you?"

Ruby looked up at him, startled. "I … maybe I am."

"Ruby, you don't have to tell me anything, if you don't want to. I'll always be your friend, no matter what. You're a good woman, and whatever happened to you doesn't change that."

"How can you say that? I've changed, Jake. And maybe not for the better either."

Jake reached over and took her hand. "Remember when we were out huntin' and found that hurt coon kit? As I recollect, your Pa was none too happy when you insisted on bringin' it home and nursing it back to health. You wouldn't back down, 'cause you saw a creature that needed your help. That's who you are, Ruby, a good, kind, smart and feisty lady. Nothing that happened to your body has changed that."

Ruby searched his face. "You really mean that, don't you? You always were my best friend."

"Hope I still am."

She nodded, falling silent. "What I went through … no girl should have to face that. It filled me with so much anger and hate that I kinda lost myself. I hated Joe and Ray, I hated the men who used me … I even hated myself for a long, long while. At least I'm startin' to not hate myself anymore." She gave a short laugh.

"Who are Joe and Ray?"

"Are you sure you want to know?"

"I'm sure I want to hear whatever you want to tell me, whatever you need me to hear to understand how it was for you."

Ruby closed her eyes for a second, gathering her thoughts, and then she began to speak. She told him about meeting Ray, what happened when she woke up at Joe's house, and how her leg had been broken and set wrong. She talked about the men coming to the house and using her and the girls, about Mary's death, and how she'd encouraged them to somehow seek out her parents. Then she told him about Doris's failed plan to get her out, about Joe's death, and about the fire that allowed her to escape. The only thing Ruby didn't talk about was the sheriff. She remembered the deal they'd made – he'd put her on the bus and she'd stay quiet about him. While it hadn't worked out as planned, what with Joe showing up, she still wanted to honor his change of heart. "Now, I'm staying with Doris until I'm ready to move on."

Jake had watched her face as she'd spoken her piece, and now, he reached over to gently wipe away the tears hanging on her eyelashes. "I won't lie and pretend I'm not shocked and horrified at what happened to you, but you got nothin' to feel ashamed about. Those things were done to your body, Ruby. Of course it affected who you are, your heart and mind, but it sounds to me like that part of you is healing too." Jake sat back in his chair and was silent for a minute. "It's a damn good thing Joe's dead!"

"What?" Her eyes widened at him in astonishment.

"If he wasn't already dead, I'd have to go find him and kill him for what he did to you."

"That's not you, any more than I could have killed him off when I was there. I thought about it, believe me, but ..." she laughed. "I guess both of us are just gentler folk than that. Or maybe we were payin' attention on Sundays when Pastor Tyree talked about lovin' our enemies."

"Not sure I'm there yet."

"Me neither. But I'm workin' on it."

Before he left for the day, Jake stopped in to see Ruby again. "I wanted to say good night before I make tracks for home. The medical boards are in two days, and it feels like I'll never be ready. There's a stack of textbooks waiting for me on my kitchen table. I know I'm not really behind the grind, but it feels like it. "

"You'll do great, Jake. I just know you will. You always were the smartest fella I knew."

"Thanks, Ruby. See ya in a few days." He started to turn away, and then asked, "How come your folks haven't shown up here yet? I'd have thought your Ma would be sittin' at your bedside by now."

"Jake, they don't know I'm here, and you can't tell them. Please … promise me you won't," she pleaded with him. "I haven't even written to let them know I'm alive. Boy, that would be some letter, wouldn't it? – *Dear Ma and Pa, I'm alive. I was a whore and now I'm not. Love, Ruby.*"

"Well, that's just dumb. You know they love you, no matter what – or at least you should know that. I think you're just afraid."

"I am afraid! Afraid I'll see rejection in their eyes. Afraid they'll be polite, all the while wishin' I'd keep movin' on. I know they love me, but … yeah, I'm afraid to see them again."

"You need to trust them. And I think, deep down, you do – why else did you tell those girls to seek them out if they could? Don't you suppose one of them by now let slip what happened to you?"

Ruby shuddered. "Lordy, I hope not!"

"Even if you won't go see them, you've got to write and let them know you're alive. They must have been sick with worry ever since you disappeared. At least give them some peace. Let them know you aren't dead." Jake was beginning to get irked with her.

"I'll think about it," Ruby replied, glaring at him.

Jake stalked out of the room, returning a few minutes later. He slapped a pen and a writing pad down on her tray table, turned and stalked out again.

Thirty-Four

SOMETIMES YOU CAN'T GO HOME

August 1934
Raleigh, North Carolina

"Drat this rain! It's makin' me feel out of sorts," Doris muttered as she went to answer the ringing of the doorbell. Yanking open the door, she beheld the bedraggled figure of a young woman, soaked to the skin by the rain. "What ..." she paused and squinted at the girl. "Anna? Is that you, honey? Get on in here, and let's get you dried off."

A short time later, Anna and Doris sat in the wingback chairs in front of the fire in the library. Anna, wrapped in a blanket, huddled in the chair. "He threw me out, Doris," she said softly, trying not to break down in tears.

"Who threw you out? Why would they do that?"

"My Pa. He said I was a scarlet woman now, and I wasn't fit to be under his roof."

"Why that ol' fool! I thought he was a preacher man. Aren't they supposed to be all about forgiveness?"

"He is a preacher, a good one too. But it seems somebody on the church board found out about me and threatened to tell the whole church I was a whore. Pa had to choose between me and his position."

"And he chose his position, the damn fool! At least take comfort in the old sayin' 'As ye sow, so shall ye reap' – this will come back to haunt the ol' hypocrite."

Anna whispered, tears spilling down her cheeks, "He said I wasn't his daughter anymore."

Doris fell to her knees in front of Anna, gathering her in her arms. "Oh, darlin', I'm so sorry. I'm so sorry. You can stay here with me for as long as you want." The rest of the conversation was lost in weeping and whispers.

Ruby had eventually been allowed to return to Doris's house to continue healing. As the stairs were too difficult for her to handle on crutches, she took up residence in the library, sleeping on a couch, and using either crutches or a wood and whicker wheelchair to get around. She hadn't meant to eavesdrop on Doris and Anna. Burrowed under a blanket on a couch pushed back in the shadows across the room, Ruby had no choice but to overhear Anna's tale, and her heart broke for the girl. Suddenly she was questioning her decision to return home. If a preacher man wouldn't accept his daughter back … maybe her parents wouldn't either. She didn't think they'd reject her, but now … now she was wondering what kind of reception she'd get. *I didn't ask for what was done to me, I had no choice in the matter. I did what I had to do to survive. Will they understand that?*

When Anna finally quieted and fell asleep in Doris's arms, the woman picked up the girl and carried her from the room. Before she left, she looked over at Ruby and nodded. Maybe five minutes later, Doris was back, coming to sit by Ruby.

"You wanted me to hear that, didn't you, Doris?"

"I did. You asked me the other day where the girls went when they left here. And I told you that most of them go back home. Which is true. Sometimes, after a rough patch or two, it works out okay. But sometimes, it's just too much for the family to deal with. Anna isn't the first girl to come back here, and she won't be the last, either."

"What will she do now?"

"Depends on her. I can get her a job in town – a maid or housekeeper, or learnin' to be a secretary. In time, she's gonna want to move on out of here, 'cause this place will keep on remindin' her of the awful things that happened to her."

Ruby picked at the blanket covering her legs. "Do you think my folks will reject me too? I couldn't bear it if they did."

"Ruby, from what you've told me about them, I feel real sure they won't. Of course, you can expect some awkward times, but … well, what's in here," she touched Ruby's head, "and what's in here," she touched Ruby over her heart, "that's changed. You're not the same person they knew before, and they'll have to get to know you again."

"What if they don't like me now?"

"Not much chance of that." Doris paused. "You know, sometimes we fear most what we want the most. Right now, what you want most is your parents' acceptance and love. But you're twistin' yourself up in knots because you're afraid to find out if they'll reject you or not."

"What if they do?"

"Then you'll deal with that just like you've dealt with everythin' else over the past few years. Your folks are not anything like Anna's Pa. The worst thing you can do right now is to cut them out of your life. Trust me, you'll regret that."

"What do you mean?"

"After I met Eli, after we were married, I was too afraid to contact my parents. I was too ashamed of my past, of what I'd been, afraid they'd reject me. And I waited too long. By the time I gathered my courage and wrote them, I found out they had both died of the Spanish flu only a few years before. I waited too long, and now I'll never know. Ruby, don't make my mistake." Doris reached out and tapped Ruby's arm. "There's somethin' else you need to think about. Sometimes, our past can show up again in our lives, sudden like. That can be good, like Jake, or … or it can be someone we hoped to never see again."

"You mean like one of the men who …."

"I do. And I think you need to ask Celine about the letter she just got from her friend, Gloria. She passed through here a little over a year ago, and … well, just ask Celine." Doris stood. "Now if you'll excuse me, I need to go talk to our new cook. With you laid up, I had to hire a fine Negro lady, Alma, to keep us fed. She's a treasure."

"I thought the girls were still takin' turns with the cookin'."

"They can help out, but some of them can't cook to save their souls." Doris laughed. "Honestly, I didn't want to risk being poisoned by their efforts."

Thirty-Five

SOMETIMES HOME'S NOT WHAT YOU EXPECT

After Doris left, Ruby sat, lost in thought. She had intended, once she was able to walk again, to make her way home, back to the farm and her folks. But now, after hearing what had happened to Anna, she was beginning to second guess her decision.

She levered herself into the wheelchair and went in search of Celine. She found her in Doris's office, seated at the desk, peering intently at some papers in front of her, a tiny set of *pince-nez* glasses perched on her nose.

"Can we talk for a minute?" Ruby asked, interrupting her concentration.

"What?" Celine snatched the glasses off her nose, and hid them on her lap. "*Oui, ma chére* ... what can I do for you?"

"Well, first off," Ruby replied, laughing, "You can stop hiding your glasses in your lap. I think they look charming on you."

"You do? I think they make me look like little old woman." Celine folded her hands on the desk top. "Did you have a question for me?"

"I do. Who's Gloria, and what happened to her?" She hesitated when Celine started to shake her head slightly. "I hope I'm not intruding here, but Doris said to ask you about a letter you'd got from her."

"It is okay. You probably should know. Gloria came to us here a year or so ago. We became close friends. And then she decided to go home to her family in Norfolk. I ... I think it would be better if you read letter. She tells it better than I do." Celine reached into the pocket of her dress, and passed a creased envelope across the desk to Ruby.

"You're sure?" she hesitated.

"*Oui*. Read."

Dearest Celine,

I hope this letter finds you well and happy. I am well, but not necessarily happy. As you can see by the postmark, I'm no longer in Norfolk. Philadelphia suits me better these days.

My family was glad to have me back. At first, they were awkward, and didn't have much to say

196

to me, but after a few weeks it got better. I honestly thought I could make a go of it here, back in what had been my hometown. I was wrong.

The problem was not my family, it was me. I got a job at Norfolk General, my old hospital, but, times being what they are, at close to half what I made before. At least I had a job. The problem was that I was spooked. I kept waiting for one of the male patients to recognize me — after all, it's less than a hundred miles between Norfolk and where I was kept.

I finally decided to head north, and I ended up here. I think I have a job in a nursing home, but I'll find out for sure tomorrow.

Though they didn't say it, I think my folks were glad I left. They love me, but could never really get comfortable with me again. It was best for me to leave.

Please write back, and let me know how you are. I think of you often. Give my love to Doris too. Love, your friend — Gloria

Ruby sat quietly, looking at the letter in her hand, deep in thought. She looked up at Celine, visibly shaken. "I hadn't thought … of that problem … that I could be walkin' down the street in Roanoke and be approached by a man who'd remember me from Joe's. I'd die right there on the spot, I really would."

Celine sighed. "It doesn't happen all that often, but it could."

"So, not only do we have to worry that our families will not want us back, but we also have to worry that we'll run into someone who …. So what do we do?"

"Everybody is different, but I would suggest that you go home. See what happens. You can always move on from there. And you know our doors here will always be open to you."

Ruby handed the letter back to Celine. "I'll think about it. Right now, it all seems pretty darn scary."

Celine smiled at her. "Did you ever write your Mama and Papa like Jake told you?"

Ruby hung her head. "Not yet. I don't know what to say."

Celine shrugged. "You can always throw the letters in the fire until one says what you need it to say."

"I'll think about it. Thanks for sharing Gloria's letter with me. I hope she does well up North."

"Me too … me too."

Thirty-Six

NO MORE CAST

October 1934
Raleigh, North Carolina

Five long months after the surgery on her leg, it was finally time to take the cast off. Ruby couldn't wait! She was ready to be rid of the heavy thing, and the hot summer weather had made her leg itch all the time.

"Hurry up, Celine. You drive like a little ol' lady." Ruby chivvied her from the back seat.

"You be quiet back there. No distracting me. So impatient! You like cat on the skittle."

"A cat on what?" Ruby was amused at Celine's latest attempt to use a slang expression.

"Oh, you know what I mean. Now be quiet – we're almost to the hospital."

When Celine rolled Ruby into his office, Dr. Franks was waiting for them. "You about ready to get that cast off, young lady? It's time to find out how everything worked. Let's head on down to the casting room and get you out of this load of plaster."

It wasn't long before Ruby was looking down at her thin, hairy, very white leg, with a long scar running along the calf. Dr. Franks peered at it intently, running his hands over the leg, and muttering to himself. Finally, he looked up and smiled. "It looks good, Ruby. It looks good. Not perfect, but still .... You ready to try it out?"

"Can I? I don't want to hurt it again."

"Just this once. Take my hand, and slowly stand and put some weight on the leg. We'll take it slow. Just a little weight on it at first. Go easy, now." Dr. Franks stood in front of Ruby as she slowly did as he asked. "Good ... good ... that's it."

Ruby grinned at him. "It feels mighty odd, but it doesn't hurt. All tingly like."

"Okay. That's as it should be. In a few weeks, I'm gonna schedule you for some therapy to get you usin' that leg again. It'll take a couple of months, too. Just take it slow, use your crutches for now. You'll graduate to usin' that fancy cane of yours soon enough. You'll do fine."

"That's about the best news I've had in a while, Doc. Words aren't enough for what you've done for me, but … thank you … a million times, thank you."

"Maybe, once you're up to it, you'll have me over to Doris's for some of your superior meatloaf? That'd be mighty appreciated."

"Count on it, Dr. Franks. We still haven't celebrated Jake passin' his medical boards either, so maybe he'll come along with you."

"When you're ready, name the date and we'll be there."

Thirty-Seven

A MISUNDERSTANDING

December 1934
Raleigh, North Carolina

A last minute emergency at the hospital meant that Jake couldn't ride out to Doris's house with Dr. Franks. Tonight was the famous 'meatloaf night' Dr. Franks swore was not to be missed. Plus, they were celebrating Jake passing his boards two months ago. He was looking forward to spending the evening with friends, and sharing with them his big news.

As Jake left the hospital building, he hailed a passing cab. Though it was a brisk early December evening, with the scent of snow in the air, the inside of the cab was warm and smelled slightly of cigarettes and worn leather. He settled back in the rear seat with a sigh, reading off the address of his destination to the driver from a paper in his hand.

"Oh ho. So you're goin' out there for a little early Christmas joy, huh? Fine lookin' fella like you should have a right fine time," the cab driver said, eyeing Jake in the cab's rear view mirror.

Jake was puzzled. "What d'you mean? I'm having supper with friends there."

"So that's what you modern fellas are callin' it these days, 'havin' dinner'?" the cabbie laughed. "Son, no matter what you call it, screwin' is still screwin', and a chippie is still a chippie. Just relax and enjoy yourself."

Jake rapidly went from puzzled to angry. "Look, I don't appreciate what you're suggesting. I'm joinin' friends there to have supper and celebrate some good news. There're no chippies involved!"

"Whoa there, young fella. No need to get that tone with me. You get into my cab and give me the address of the most uppity whorehouse in town, and you expect me to buy that you're goin' there just for food? I got my doubts about that," the driver answered back gruffly.

"What do you mean a whorehouse? That's the address I was given." Jake looked at the piece of paper again, and repeated the address to the driver.

"Yeah. That's the place," the man nodded.

"But that can't be. That's where a friend of mine lives, a girl I've known since we were kids. She's not ... at least I didn't think .... No, there must be some mistake. She can't be a whore!"

"Son, I don't know what she told you, but if she's livin' in a whorehouse, I'd be thinkin' she is one. She probably has her reasons for lyin' to you about that – women do that, you know."

Jake found himself becoming angry with Ruby. He hoped the driver was wrong, but now he had his doubts. "I hope you're wrong. We'll see. So what do you know about this house?"

The cabbie grinned. "I've never been there, you understand. I heard it's a classy joint, way too high class for me. You have to be invited to go there." For the rest of the trip, the man regaled Jake with rumors about what went on at Doris's house. By the time they arrived, Jake was furious, pretty much convinced that Ruby had lied to him. Why, he wasn't sure, but he aimed to find out.

Ruby watched Jake slam the cab's door and stand watching the cab disappear down the drive. She guessed by the set of his shoulders that he was angry, and when he turned to face her, the look on his face confirmed that.

"What's wrong, Jake? Did something happen at the hospital?" Ruby waited for him on the porch, leaning on her cane.

"You. Tell. Me." Jake enunciated angrily. "The cabbie had some very interesting stories to tell me on the ride out here. Seems like I'm having supper in a very famous whorehouse. Were you gonna tell me, or just spring it on me?"

"This place is much more than that. This is where I live. I told you what Doris does, how she finds women who've had it rough and gives them a place to be safe again."

"Oh, you told me about that. But you didn't tell me about the whorehouse side of things. You lied to me!"

"Jacob Boone! You get up here on this porch, right now! If I'm gonna fight with you, it'll be face to face!" She stomped her cane on the porch. "I never lied to you! Never!"

"Really?" Jake asked sarcastically, as he took the porch steps two at a time.

"Yes, really!"

"So you're sayin' this isn't a whorehouse, and you're not a whore?"

Ruby hauled off and slapped him so hard his head snapped back. "You stupid man! Do you think you can insult me by callin' me a whore?" She snorted. "Some of the finest women I know are whores. And some of the worst men I know are those fine upstandin' men who think nothin' of usin' a whore for their fun."

"So is this a whorehouse or not?"

"Part of it is. But most of it …"

Jake interrupted her. "Then you lied to me!"

"I did not!"

"You did! You said that you weren't a whore. If you live in a whorehouse, then you gotta be a whore. After what you went through, how could you …."

Through gritted teeth, Ruby ground out, "Let me say this slowly, so even a stupid man like you can understand. I. Am. Not. A. Whore!"

"Ruby, women who aren't whores don't live in whorehouses, they just don't. Unless maybe they're the cook." Jake paused. "Is that it? Are you the cook?"

"Ah … finally you're thinkin' with that big head of yours. As a matter of fact, I was the cook here, until I got laid up by the surgery."

"Then you're not …."

"No, Jake, I'm not. Everything I told you was true. Everything that happened to me was real. I thought you understood. I'm not sure why you're suddenly findin' that so hard to believe. I guess I misjudged you." She turned to go into the house. "I'll call you another cab. You can sit out here on the porch till it comes if you want."

Jake sank down into a porch rocker. Head in his hands, he said softly, "Ruby, why do you stay here now? Doesn't being around all that make it hard for you … the memories and all?"

She paused, her hand on the door. "At first, I thought it would, but, oddly enough, it hasn't. I'm guessin' it's 'cause the few girls who work that side of the house do so by choice. They're not forced into anything. They choose."

"I guess that makes some sense."

"Livin' here, I've learned a lot from the other women, about courage and honor and dignity. I think I finally have the courage to take control of my life again. I wrote my folks two weeks ago askin' if I could come home for Christmas. Heard back today – they want to come and get me. You were right about that, at least."

"I'm glad you got in touch with them."

"Hopefully, they won't judge me as harshly as you did."

"Ruby, I'm sorry about that. I was wrong. I should have known better, but …"

"But what?" She broke in.

"God, I'm such an ass! I was so shocked when the cabbie called this a whorehouse. I honestly didn't know, and it caught me by surprise. And then he assumed I was going here to be with a whore. He told me all kinds of stories about what he thinks goes on here, and … well, I got confused, and angry. Wondered if maybe you hadn't been completely honest with me, and then I got embarrassed at what the cabbie was assuming about me and about you, and … well … my big mouth started sayin' stupid things."

"That it did!"

"Ruby, I truly do know you're not a whore, not now, not ever."

"That's not what you said a few minutes ago. Why were you so mad at me?"

"I guess I really wasn't mad at you, I was mad at the cabbie for what he said, and I was mad at myself for halfway believing him. It was easier to get mad at you."

Ruby turned back to look at him. "Seems like you got some things to work out."

"You're right, I guess I do. I'm sorry. Sorry for what I said. Sorry I hurt you."

"It did hurt. But I guess I gotta get used to it. People will always be gettin' on their high horses and jumpin' to judgement. We've been friends for ages, so I just expected you'd do better. Know this, Jacob Boone – I will never again feel shame for what was done to me."

"Do you still want me to go?" he asked softly.

"That depends. Are you gonna be an ass or not? Do you still think I lied to you?"

"No, I don't think you lied to me. And yes, I'll try real hard not to be an ass."

"Okay then, you can stay, but you better be on your best behavior."

"Yes, ma'am!" He gently fingered the red handprint still evident on his face. "You still pack a wallop, you know."

"Serves you right! Now come on – don't want supper to get cold."

Thirty-Eight

PLANS

Dr. Franks sighed, leaning back in his chair and tugging at his suspenders. "You outdid yourself again, my dear," he said to Ruby.

She laughed. "I thank you kindly, but the only thing I made was the meatloaf. Everythin' else was done by Alma."

"Well, it was a fine meatloaf, that's for sure."

Only Doris, Celine and Ruby joined Dr. Franks and Jake for supper. Having filled up on meatloaf, mashed potatoes and greens, they relaxed around the table over cups of chicory-flavored coffee.

"Ruby?" Jake asked, "When are your folks gonna get here?"

"Well, that's the thing – they're not." She held up her hand to stop what he'd been about to say. "I asked them not to. I've been thinkin' about it, and it's real important to me to **go** home, not be **taken** there."

"*Oui*, that is wise. Be in control, as you would say?"

"Yes, that's exactly right. I know they're anxious to see me, but I gotta do this my way."

"So, what are you goin' to do?" Jake asked.

"I'll be leavin' here around the eighteenth or nineteenth." She gave a crooked grin. "Gonna get up my courage and take a bus to Roanoke. They'll meet me there."

"Are you sure you want to do that, Ruby?" Doris asked. "I'd be glad to give you the extra money for a train ticket so you don't have to get on a bus again."

"I thank you for that, but … I know it probably doesn't make much sense, but I feel like I gotta get back on a bus. Face my fears, I guess."

"You will do fine, Ruby." Celine patted her hand. "Probably you will fear it more before than when you really get on the bus."

"I hope you're right. My head knows it's silly to feel almost frozen at the idea of getting' on a bus, but the butterflies in my stomach are tellin' a different story. I just feel it's an important step for me."

Jake spoke up. "Maybe I can help you out here. See, I'm goin' back to Roanoke about then too. I had planned to take the train, but I could just as well take the bus. Then I could ride along with you, as backup, moral support ... or I could just be invisible. Whatever you want."

"Jake, that's mighty swell of you. Let me think on it, okay?"

"Sure, just let me know."

"Jake, does that mean you heard back?" Dr. Franks asked.

Grinning at the puzzled looks on the others' faces, Jake said, "I did. First, I better explain. I applied to do my residency at two different hospitals, and I heard back today. I got accepted at the new Salem Veterans' Medical Center in Roanoke."

"You mean the one I read about in the newspaper? The one that FDR just helped dedicate back in October? That one?" At his nod, Ruby clapped her hands and grinned at him. "Your folks will be right happy to have you back. When do you start?"

"I have to be there the first week of January, so I'm plannin' to spend Christmas with the family first." Jake laughed and rubbed his ear. "When I called Ma with the news, she yelled so loud it nigh unto broke my ear drum."

"Looks like we'll be two prodigals returning for Christmas." Ruby made a quick decision. "In that case, I think it would be right for us to ride the bus together. Seems kinda fated, doesn't it?"

While Ruby and Jake discussed their travel plans, Dr. Franks talked quietly with Doris and Celine. "I'm gonna miss those two. It's been a real pleasure havin' a hand in teachin' him and watchin' him take fire."

"Same here. Ruby is one of the strongest women I know. One of the best. It won't be the same around here without her. I know you will miss her terribly too." This last was directed at Celine.

"She is like a sister to me. I don't want her to leave, but I am happy she is better in here," Celine tapped her chest. "Now she can start to live again."

Ruby overheard what Celine was saying, and broke into the conversation. "Celine, you are the sister of my heart. If it hadn't been for you and Doris, I don't think I would have survived. I know for sure I wouldn't have been able to put these awful years behind me and move on. I owe you both my sanity … my life."

"It's not going to be easy," cautioned Doris, "but you know that. Anytime you need us, we're here for you."

"Or maybe I come see you sometime?" Celine asked.

"I'd like that! Very much. There's no phone at my folks' place, but if I need to, I can call from town. Thank you for that."

"I think this evening calls for me to open the bottle of port I was savin' for Christmas. We have two new futures to celebrate." Doris got the bottle of wine from the sideboard, and for the rest of the evening, the five friends talked and laughed, reminiscing in the way of friends who knew they would soon be parted.

The day before Ruby was to leave, she went in search of Doris. She found her fussing over a vase of flowers in the sitting room of the brothel side of the house.

"I can't seem to get these flowers put right," Doris said as Ruby walked in. "You any better at this than I am?"

Ruby laughed. "Never got the hang of it. They look fine to me." She sat on the sofa, patting a spot near her. "Can we talk?"

"Sure. What's on your mind?" Doris sat.

"I want to ask you to do something, for me, for you. I want you to …" Ruby gestured around the room. "I'm askin' you to give some serious consideration to closing down this side of your house."

"I told you before that this side helps pay for what I can do for the girls. I need the extra money to be able to …"

Ruby interrupted her. "I understand that. But I'm still askin' you to shut it down, and trust that somethin' else will come along. You could start a business of some kind, or even try to invest some of your husband's money."

Doris grimaced. "These days?"

"Yes, even these days. You've told me many times to believe in myself, to trust myself. I'm askin' you to do the same. Trust in yourself, Doris."

"I'll think about it, but …"

"This side reminds the girls of what they went through. It slows down their healin'. It's hard to move on when … well, this side says to them that tradin' sex for money is okay."

Doris looked startled. "I hadn't thought of it like that."

"And I think it reminds you of your past too. You left that behind. Let go of it. I noticed you don't join us when we write and burn things. Maybe you should, 'cause I don't think you've made peace with your past yet."

Doris was quiet, holding herself ridged. She sighed, her shoulders slumping. "You may have a point. In fact, you've given me a couple of things to think about." She stood. "I can't promise I'll shut this side down. But I will think on what you've said."

Ruby stood, giving Doris a hug. "That's all I ask. Those flowers look fine, leave them be. It's almost time for supper, anyway. You comin'?"

"I'll be there in a minute." After Ruby left, Doris stood looking around the sitting room, lost in thought.

The morning of December eighteenth dawned clear but cold. Ruby and Jake stood with Doris and Celine in the waiting room of the Greyhound station. Ruby was wearing the coat Celine had given her, and her new shoulder bag was a gift from Doris. She shifted nervously from foot to foot, leaning on her cane, and trying not to think about the trip ahead of her. There were last minute hugs and tears, and then it was time for the two travelers to get on the bus.

Jake quietly offered Ruby his arm, and she gratefully put her trembling hand on it. When they stepped outside and she saw the bus, she stopped dead in her tracks.

"Maybe I should take the train," she said breathlessly, sweat beading her forehead despite the December chill.

"You can do this. I'm right here with you." Jake whispered back. "Take a deep breath. And imagine the hugs you're gonna get when we get there."

Ruby took a shaky breath and looked up at him. "You're a good friend, Jake Boone. Thank you for comin' with me." Biting her lip and clutching his arm, Ruby walked up to the waiting bus. Gathering her courage, she boarded it, taking a window seat near the driver. When Jake sat beside her, she gave him a shaky smile. "I did it!"

"That you did. I'm proud of you, ya know."

Ruby waved at Doris and Celine who returned her wave before turning away. The bus's brakes released with a heavy sigh, and it began rolling down the street.

Thirty-Nine

HOMECOMING

December 1934
Roanoke, Virginia
Ruby looked out the window of the bus as the familiar landscape of Roanoke came into view. Her stomach was so full of butterflies, she thought she'd be sick for sure. She reached over and took Jake's hand. "I'm scared," she said softly.

"I know you are." Jake squeezed her hand before releasing it. "I wish I could say some magical words and make everything hunky-dory. If I were a magician like Harry Houdini, that'd be no problem, but …. Just be yourself, and trust they love you."

Within minutes, the Greyhound pulled up at the new bus station in Roanoke. It gave Ruby some comfort that she didn't have to get off the bus by the diner, like she had that night two years ago. As they gathered their things, she looked out and saw both their sets of parents waiting in front of the station.

219

As Ruby stepped off the bus, she heard her Ma call out her name. All Ruby could do was drop her bags on the ground, and tearfully respond, "Ma?" before she was engulfed in a fierce hug. Both of her folks surrounded her, holding on as if she'd disappear again.

"Don't cry, baby girl. You're home now," Lida Malcolm said, reaching up to wipe the tears off Ruby's cheeks. That just made Ruby cry more, ducking her head onto Lida's shoulder.

After a minute or two, Ruby pulled herself together, with a visible effort. "Sorry 'bout that. I wasn't expectin' to fall apart like …"

Tom Malcolm silenced his daughter with a wave of his hand. "Nothin' to be sorry for, child. I'd blubber too, 'cept I cry ugly." Pleased he'd coaxed a small grin out of Ruby, he continued, "Let us say hello to Jake quick like, and then we can head home."

Ruby watched as her folks shook Jake's hand and stood talking to him. *I sure hope they don't make a big deal of the fact we came on the same bus. If our mothers start to matchmaking, I'll just have to nip that in the bud.*

When Ruby bent to pick up her bags, Tom beat her to it, scooping them up. "I'll get those." He nodded at the cane she was leaning on. "You got enough to handle. That's a fancy stick you got there."

"That it is, Pa. A good friend gave it to me."

"You can tell me all about that later on. Let's get you home first."

As Ruby and her folks rounded the corner of the station, she noticed a young woman lounging against the side of their car. Something about her seemed familiar, but … "Della? Is that really you?" They both burst into tears, clinging to each other.

Tom rolled his eyes and grinned. "Ladies, ladies … waterworks in the car, please," and he shooed them into the backseat, as he stowed Ruby's bags in the trunk. "Glad I brought a couple of extra handkerchiefs. Thought me might need 'em," he added, passing two large white handkerchiefs over the seat back to Della and Ruby. The rest of the ride to the farm was quiet. No one seemed to want to start a conversation in case they touched on something painful.

When Tom finally parked the car in front of the farmhouse, the first thing Ruby noticed was the addition. "You added a room on to the house. I thought you were savin' up to do some work on the barn."

"We were, but that's gotta wait for now. We couldn't have the girls who stopped by sleepin' on the floor, now could we?" Lida shrugged, smiling over the back of the seat. "Della helped us figure it out. You'll see." With that, she got out of the car and headed for the house.

"Wait! Ma … Pa … there's so much I need to tell you. I …"

"No, young lady." Tom gestured for her to go ahead of him. "Right now, you need to unpack and settle in. Take a bath if you want. Ma and Della will finish up supper, and we can talk all you want after that."

As Ruby was unpacking her suitcase, Della came into her room and plopped down on the bed, watching her. "Della, how much do they know?"

"Pretty much everythin'." Seeing her friend blanch, Della added, "I didn't say much, but we've had four girls come through here in the past six months. Each one praised you to high heaven, and each one kinda added to what your folks were already figurin' out. One night, they sat me down and told me what they were guessin' at. They had some things all wrong, so I had to set them straight, Ruby. I'm sorry if you're mad at me now."

"No, I'm not mad. I'd have liked to be the one who told them what happened to me, but I think maybe, on some level, I was also hopin' the girls would come here and kinda soften up Ma and Pa. Does that make sense?"

"Yeah, it does. Anyway, you don't need to be worryin' about talkin' to your folks. They'll just try to smother you with hugs and make it all better."

Ruby turned back to her unpacking. "So Ma has you cookin' now?"

"She's teachin' me, so I don't poison anybody by accident. In fact, I made the biscuits for supper …" Della paused, a horrified look crossing her face. "Oh no – the biscuits!" and she dashed out of the room.

Forty

REVELATIONS

Supper was an awkward affair, with Ruby mostly just pushing the food around on her plate. Normally she'd enjoy the ham with the green beans her Ma had canned the summer before. Even Della's biscuits had turned out fine. This evening, Ruby was too worried about talking to her folks to do it justice.

Clearing her throat, Della put down her fork and asked, "Who's this Jake fella you got off the bus with? What's he to you?"

Ruby grinned at her. "Why, I've known Jake pretty much all my life. We grew up together 'round here. We met up again down in Raleigh."

"Where did y'all meet up down there?" Lida wanted to know.

"He was an orderly in the hospital where I had the surgery on my leg. He was studyin' to take the medical boards, and he was workin' with Dr. Franks, my doctor."

"So did y'all see a lot of each other?" Lida raised her eyebrows as she asked.

"Some. Jake'd come by my room when he could, and we'd talk about books and the people we knew. Stuff like that. But Ma ... you can put those matchmakin' ideas clean out of your head." As Lida started to protest, Ruby continued, "We've both changed a lot. He's now a respectable doctor, and I'm ... I'm Ruby, the fallen woman."

"No!" Tom slapped the table with his hand, making the dishes jump. "You will not talk about yourself like that in this house. You did nothin' wrong, and I ..."

Putting her hand on his arm, Ruby interrupted him. "I know you've heard a lot about what all happened to me. But maybe you should hear it from me."

Della started to stand up. "I'll just leave y'all alone."

"Please, stay. It'd be a comfort to me if you did." Ruby nodded as Della sat back down. She drew a deep breath and let it out slowly. "I got on the bus in Norfolk, just as we planned."

For the next two hours, Ruby talked, telling her folks about her ordeal. She told them about Joe and Ray, about the other girls, and about ... well, about most everything. She left out Sheriff Atlee's involvement. He'd had a change of heart and tried to put her on a bus. Even though it didn't work out, she still felt she owed him for that.

"She saved us, you know," added Della. "She took care of us, and made us feel we were worth something, even in that hell." Della smiled crookedly through the tears in her eyes.

As dusk deepened into dark, the kerosene lamps were lit. At some point, Tom brought out a bottle of 'shine, filling four glasses almost to the brim. Still, Ruby talked. She told them about the fire and seeing Joe die.

"Good riddance to bad rubbish," Tom muttered.

Still, Ruby talked. She told them about Doris and the house in Raleigh, which even Della knew nothing about. She talked about trying to make peace with what had happened. And she told them about Dr. Franks and what he'd done for her.

"I've still got some therapy to do, and I may be usin' my fancy cane from here on out, but it's much, much better." Ruby looked at the tear-streaked faces of her folks. "And now you know what happened. I'd understand if you didn't want me to stay here, really I would."

"I've just got one question." Tom reached over and took Ruby's hand. "Why didn't you write to us sooner? We'd have come and got you. You didn't have to spend all that time tryin' to patch yourself back together on your own."

"I lost count of the number of letters I started writin' to you. But then I'd chicken out and tear them up. I didn't know what to say ... how to tell you what had happened. And then I heard stories from other girls who'd tried to go home and it didn't work out .... I was scared. I wanted to beg forgiveness, and ask you to come get me. But I had to take control of my life again. I could **come** home, but not be **taken** there. Does that make sense?"

Lida scooted over to sit next to Ruby on the bench seat. "It does, though I can't say it didn't hurt some to find out from others that you were alive and didn't feel you could come home."

"I'm sorry, Ma."

"I'm just glad to have you back, baby girl."

Tom stood abruptly. "You got nothin' to beg forgiveness for, not from us, not from nobody." He headed for the door, taking one of the lanterns with him.

"Where you goin', Pa?" Lida asked.

"Woodpile," he answered, shutting the door behind him.

"What?" Ruby looked at Lida questioningly.

"When he gets riled up, your Pa has found peace in choppin' up a mess of wood."

"But it's dark out there. He'll miss the wood and hit his leg if he's not real careful!" Della shook her head.

"Which is why I'll let you girls see to cleanin' up after supper, and I'll go out there and supervise. Dang fool didn't even take his coat, and it's December!"

Forty-One

NAMES ON A LIST

"Ruby, we sure are glad to see you back here." Sheriff Carter shook Ruby's hand before she perched gingerly on the edge of a chair in front of his desk. Tom and Ruby had come into town to talk to the sheriff and fill him in on their daughter's return. "Your Pa tells me you have some things to tell me about."

"Yes, sir, I do. I was on a bus from Norfolk, two years ago, when I met a man." Comforted by her Pa's presence in the chair next to hers, she once more began to relate what had happened to her. Jasper let her talk, not asking questions till she was done.

"That pretty much confirms what Della told us too. Sounds like their operation is done, what with the fire and all, but I'd sure like to try to track down the last brother. From what you say, seems like Joe dyin' was an accident. Don't know that we could prove it wasn't after the time that's passed though."

229

"He looked dead to me, and there was a good amount of blood under his head. Could be it makes me hard-hearted, but as long as he's dead, I'm happy."

"I can understand that. Sure would like to catch up to Ray though. He's got a lot to answer for. You got any idea what his last name is? That'd help. It's nigh unto impossible to track somebody down with only a first name."

"They were real cagey 'bout that. They'd say it was 'Smith', but then they'd laugh." Ruby sighed. "I know the place was near Dalton, I saw a ... a sticker on a car one time, but that's about it."

Jasper nodded. "I talked to the sheriff in Dalton. He said he found a burned out old house up in the hills, but no sign of anybody havin' been there in a while. So that proved to be another dead end. He did say he'd keep an eye out for Ray, but it doesn't look good."

At the mention of the Dalton sheriff, Ruby stopped listening. *I don't know what to do. I should tell about that man's part in everything. But he decided to do the right thing, he tried to put me on a bus home. If Joe hadn't shown up when he did ... not really Atlee's fault what Joe did to me after that. I feel I owe him for trying. It doesn't hurt nothing to keep quiet about him, but ....*

"Ruby," Jasper broke into her thoughts, "I'd like you to take a look at this Missing Persons' Report and tell me if you recognize any of the names. Maybe they were there at that house with you. Might help us figure out what happened to some of them." He pushed a sheet of paper across the desk to her. "The circled ones are the young women."

Ruby took the list off the desk and scanned the names he'd circled. "That one there – Margaret McLeod. She was at the house. I remember her – she told the best stories."

"You know what happened to her?"

"Not really. Just that one day she got sold on. Don't know to where." Ruby pointed to another circled name. "There was a Dora there for a little bit. She never said what her last name was. I remember she had big blue eyes though, and she cried a lot. Most of them did, at least at first." Ruby looked at the sheriff, visibly shaken. "I'm sorry. I know that doesn't help much."

"That's okay. Every little bit helps. I know it must be hurtful goin' over those memories. I thank you for doin' that. Feels like we're graspin' at straws here, but that's about all we can do." The sheriff stood up. "If you think of anythin' else, you let me know. Meantime, you enjoy the pamperin' I know your Ma's heapin' on you."

Forty-Two

CHRISTMAS

Tromping around in the woods, looking for the perfect Christmas tree, had always been one of Ruby's favorite things about Christmas. There was something about the hunt for that one special tree that made her smile from ear to ear. They'd been searching for an hour now, but every tree that Della or Pa suggested was just too green, or too perfect for Ruby. She wasn't sure what she was looking for, but she figured she'd know it when she found it. And then … there it was, five feet tall, dead on one side, and looking rather the worse for wear. To Ruby, it was perfect.

"Over here. I found it!" she called out.

When they reached her, Della and Pa just looked at the tree. Head cocked, scratching his head, Tom asked, "This one? You sure?"

"Yeah, I'm sure. Poor thing'll be dead by spring, most likely. Might as well let it go out in style."

Della laughed. "You got a point."

Later, when they presented their find to Lida, she just shook her head and handed them a Sears catalog she'd been saving. "We'll need some paper chains and snowflakes," she ordered.

That night after supper, they transformed the sad little ugly duckling of a tree into a swan. They draped it in colorful paper chains and snowflakes, while Tom added the wooden ornaments he'd carved over the years. Ruby recognized most of them from her childhood, but there were several new ones, too. She was fingering one of them, a delicate star, when Tom put his hand on her shoulder. "I made a special one each year you were missing – each of them a star to guide you home."

"Thank you!" she whispered as she leaned against him.

Christmas morning dawned bright and clear, not a snowflake or raindrop in sight. Lida and Tom gave each of the girls an orange and the new aprons that Lida had made for them. Ruby and Della exchanged the scarves they had made for each other, dissolving in laughter when they realized they both had been up late into the night knitting to finish their gifts.

When she could finally talk without lapsing into giggles again, Ruby turned to her folks. "Our gift to you is a day off. When we get back from church, you just set yourselves down. We'll be takin' care of everythin' that needs doin' today."

As Lida started to protest, Della chimed in. "It's the least we can do. Sit on the porch, go fishin' or somethin'. We'll put supper on the table."

Tom grinned. "I like that. Get your coats, ladies. Pastor Tyree'll fuss at us if we're late. After service, you girls can take over. Not sure I won't twitch a bit 'cause I'm not good at sittin' still, but I'll give it a try."

It was, Ruby thought as she drifted off to sleep that night, the best Christmas she could remember. After the church service, they'd returned to the house, where they sat out on the front porch playing card games and I Spy. They all knew the warm Christmas Day weather wouldn't last, so they made the most of it. Ruby and Della cooked a fine supper of roast chicken, cornbread, and kale fresh from the garden. The oranges they portioned out as dessert. They ended the day singing around the tree, accompanied by Tom on his harmonica. It had been a perfect day, and Ruby fell asleep with a smile on her face.

Forty-Three

RUBY IS RECOGNIZED

January 1935
Roanoke, Virginia

Ruby carefully guided Tom's truck through the snow covered streets of town. A storm had dropped an inch of snow the night before, and the nip in the air promised more snow soon. Ruby wanted to get her errand done and be home before then. Her luck held, and she found a parking place at the curb in front of the train station. She was there to pick up the remnants of her life in Norfolk. When her school had been closed in 1932, she'd been given a week to pack up her classroom. Not an easy task! Books, toys, art supplies, all the things she'd scrounged up for her classroom, had been packed into boxes. Hard to believe that five years of her life had fit into seven good-sized boxes. Ruby wasn't sure what she'd do with the things packed in the boxes now, but she was grateful to Mrs. Parker, first for letting her store the boxes in the boardinghouse basement, and second for sending them to her.

235

When Ruby entered the train station, the first person she saw was the sheriff, leaning against a pillar. "Sheriff Carter," she called out, approaching him. "It's good to see you again. I want to thank you again for helping my folks try to find me when I went missin'."

"Don't think I did much to help really, Ruby. You ended up gettin' home on your own. Your folks were mighty worried about you." He straightened as she neared, and shook her hand.

"I know. Well, I'm just glad to be home."

"So, what brings you to the train station today?" Carter asked.

"Just pickin' up some boxes from Norfolk. My landlady there was keepin' some things for me, some of my personal things, and things from my classroom. Now that I'm home, she could send them on to me."

Sheriff Carter nodded. "Speakin' of classrooms, I sure was sorry to hear you'd lost your job back then. I know money's tight, but messin' with the schools just seems wrong. You thinkin' of goin' back to teachin'?"

"Maybe. I haven't decided what I'll do."

"Well, if you do want to get back in the classroom, I'd be glad to put in a good word for you."

"Thank you, Sheriff. I do appreciate that."

At the baggage office, a porter loaded Ruby's boxes onto a trolley, and followed her out of the station to put them into the bed of the truck. She held the door for the porter as he pushed the empty trolley back into the station. A man hurried out the door as she turned back to the truck.

"Hey – I know you. You were one of the girls at Joe's place, weren't you?" The man stopped and looked closely at her.

Ruby stepped back, startled. "I … I have no idea what you're talkin' about."

"Sure you do, honey. You workin' here in town now?" He leered at her.

"Look, mister, I never seen you before, and I got no idea who this 'Joe' is either. You have me mixed up with somebody else." She moved closer to the truck.

"I'd have sworn I'd seen you at Joe's … but that gal was a cripple … called her 'Gimp' we did." He looked at her, confusion on his face.

"You got it wrong, mister. Never seen you before." With that, Ruby climbed into the truck and drove away. About a mile down the road, she pulled off into a parking lot and sat till she could stop shaking. *I guess Celine's friend was right, you can't go home again*, she thought. *If that one man, against all odds, could recognize me, could remember me, then there could be more. Maybe come next spring, I will need to move on, to someplace far enough away where no one has ever heard of Joe or Dalton.*

Ruby was lost in thought as she resumed her drive home. It had started to snow while she'd been stopped, and the warm air blowing from the truck's heater was a welcome relief. A couple of blocks past the bus station, as she neared the edge of town, she saw someone walking along the side of the road. As she got closer, she could see that it was a woman, wearing a coat much too thin for the weather. Ruby stopped the truck alongside the woman, and leaned over to roll down the side window. "You need a lift? It's too cold out here dressed like you are."

"I'd be mighty grateful," the woman answered, clambering into the truck and rolling the window back up. "My name's Alice. Do you know where the Malcolm farm is? That's where I'm headed."

Ruby just stared at her for a few seconds, and then started to laugh. "Yeah, I do know where that is. Just happens I'm headed there too." She shook hands with the woman. "Nice to meet you, Alice. My name's Ruby … Ruby Malcolm." Moments later, Ruby swung the truck around and pulled up in front of the Woolworths she'd just passed. "You just sit tight, and I'll be right back. There's somethin' I think we'll be needin' that I can get here."

Ruby returned ten minutes later and set a bag on the seat. Alice looked into the bag. "That's a lotta notebooks there."

"Yeah. I got a dozen. Plus some pencils. I'm thinkin' we'll be needin' them."

"Whatever for?"

"You'll see … you'll see."

Forty-Four

A VETERAN'S STORY

April 1935
Roanoke, Virginia

A couple of weeks after they both came home to Roanoke, Jake began to occasionally come out to the Malcolm's farm for Sunday dinner. It gave Ruby and Jake a chance to reconnect as old friends, and many semi-truthful stories were told and retold. The girls who stayed at the farm came to regard Jake as an older brother of sorts. Because he was Ruby's friend, and because he was a doctor, even the girls who had the most cause to be skittish of men accepted his presence. Once in a while, he'd bring someone from the hospital with him, usually an ambulatory patient who needed to get out of the hospital for a while and breathe air not tinged with chemicals and pain.

Jake loved his job as a resident at the Salem Veteran's Medical Center in Roanoke, but sometimes the enormity of the injuries he saw weighed his spirits down. This particular Wednesday was a beautiful spring day, sunny and already warm at 7am, but Jake

240

found it hard to work up any enthusiasm for going to the hospital. It was the anniversary of his brother Sam's death fifteen years ago in the closing days of the Great War. It had been a long time, but it was never an easy day for him.

Jake stopped into the Bluebird Diner on his way to work, hoping that another cup of coffee would do the trick. He was sitting at the counter staring at his cup of coffee when Tom Malcolm sat down next to him.

"Mornin', Jake. What's got you lookin' so glum?" Tom signaled the waitress for his own cup of joe. He glanced at the calendar on the wall. "Oh. Thinkin' about Sam, huh?"

"Yeah. Can't help but think he shouldn't have gone in the first place."

"That was his call. As I recollect, he felt real strong about goin'. Nothin' you could have done to change that ." He took a sip of his coffee. "How's it goin' out at the hospital?"

"It's been rough lately, Mr. Malcolm."

"How come? I thought, since Salem's a new veterans' hospital, you'd have all the fancy equipment you need out there."

"We do, but ... sometimes," Jake confided in Tom, "sometimes I just don't know what to do for the men. I can fix their bodies, but their minds, their hearts ... their souls, that's another story."

"That's the hardest to fix, as we know from the girls."

"I guess you do. I get patients who came back from the war, and their lungs are failing them now, after some fifteen years. And there's not a whole lot I can do for them."

"They been gassed?" At Jake's nod, Tom grimaced. "I had a cousin that happened to – didn't last more than five years after comin' home. Wicked stuff!"

"That it is! But the saddest cases I see are the men with shell shock. What they heard and saw over there made them jumpy, and their minds aren't right. It's been a good long while, but that doesn't seem to matter. We do what we can, but it doesn't seem to be enough."

"You're doin' everythin' you can for the men, so don't feel you're lettin' them down." Changing the subject, Tom asked, "You comin' out to the house Sunday for dinner?" At Jake's nod he continued, "Bring one of your fellas along again. Seems to do them good."

"Thanks, Mr. Malcolm, I will. I gotta get over to the hospital now – no rest for the weary. Thanks for listenin' to me."

"Feel a mite better?"

"Yeah, I guess I do."

"Good! See ya Sunday."

Sunday rolled around, and Jake showed up with a man he introduced as Wilhelm Dietrich. "Will fought in the Great War. On our side," he hastened to add, with a laugh. Will looked to be in his late 40s, but when asked, he confided that he'd just turned 36.

"Son, hope you don't mind me sayin' it, but you look rode hard and put up wet," Tom said with a shake of his head.

Will laughed at the expression. "Guess you could say that. It was pretty grim over there. I got gassed more than once, and saw some things I wish I could un-see. But I was one of the lucky ones - I made it back." Will's voice was raspy.

"I remember readin' somethin' in a newspaper a while back – about some veterans marchin' on Washington. You know anythin' about that?" Lida asked Will.

"I do – I was there. Look, don't believe half of what you read about that mess. We went there, peaceful-like, to ask the government about the bonuses the vets were promised – could we have them now, when we really need them, and not in ten years like the government wanted. Since so many of us are out of work these days, it seemed like a reasonable request. But Hoover set the military on us. Burnt us out, sent in the cavalry, shot at us, and threw tear gas at women and children. It was shameful." Will started coughing, his breath coming in painful-sounding wheezes. It took him a couple of minutes to catch his breath again.

Lida waited for him to regain his breath. "But the papers said the marchers were Communists and the like, tryin' to start somethin' and overthrow the government."

"Not so! There were some Commie veterans there, I'll allow that. But they mostly kept to themselves. Hoover just wanted us gone, so he sent McArthur to clear us out."

"So what brought you to the veterans' hospital here in Roanoke? If it's not too personal," Della asked.

"Well, I'd been gassed during the war, chlorine gas, and I've had problems with my lungs ever since. The tear gas they fired at us in Washington really tore me up, and my lungs just can't keep up. I'm getting' some treatment here, and then they're gonna send me on up to Asheville for the mountain air. I'm not exactly a lunger, but darn close, so the doctors are hoping that will help."

"Hope so too! If nothin' else, Asheville's a right pretty place." Lida stood. "Y'all come to the table now. The biscuits should be about done, and I don't know about you, but I'm hungry."

Forty-Five

DELLA'S PAST RESURFACES

Della pushed open the door to the Piggy Wiggly with her shoulder, her arms around a heavy bag of groceries. Squinting in the bright sunlight, she didn't see the man on the sidewalk until she ran into him.

"Ooof! Sorry 'bout that, mister," she said.

"Not a problem, darlin'. You can bump into me any time you want." The man laughed, reaching out to steady Della as she shifted the bag in her arms. "What the hell!" he exclaimed, getting a good look at her face for the first time. "What are you doin' here, Della?"

Della gasped as she took a step back. "Never thought I'd have the misfortune to see you again, Beau." She tried to push past him. "Get outta my way!"

"Not so fast!" Holding her in place, he walked around her, looking her up and down. "You're lookin' good, babe … real good."

"Let me go, Beau. I got nothin' to say to you."

"Is that any way to talk to your old beau? I'm gonna think you ain't happy to see me, you keep that up."

"And you'd be right. Now let me go."

"Nah – I think we'll just move this reunion someplace else, someplace where you can show me how happy you are to see me."

"I'll scream!"

"Will ya now? Doubt that. You wouldn't want all these fine folks hereabouts to know where you been for the past year or so, now would you? Or what you been doin'?" He leered at her, tugging on her arm to get her to follow him.

Della yanked her arm free, turning back to the store. Beau grabbed her shoulder, and Della spun back, hitting him in the side of the head with the grocery bag. The bag broke open, spilling cans and a five pound bag of flour onto the ground. The bag of flour broke open, showering Beau and Della with white powder.

Bleeding from a gash on his temple, Beau lunged for Della. "You bitch! I'll make you regret that!"

"I don't think so!" Jake stepped between the pair, pushing Della behind him.

"You stay outta this, mister. This is between me and the chippie." Hands on his hips, Beau glared at Jake.

"Wrong. Once you tried to force her to go with you … then it became my business too. By now, somebody has most likely called the sheriff, so you might want to skedaddle, unless you want to try to explain all this to him."

Beau blustered. "Be glad to warn him about this chippie."

Della waved her fist at him. "You might want to think again. I bet the law would be real interested in your part in how I ended up where I did. You do remember that, don't you? I sure do."

The man stalked off, and Jake turned to Della. "Are you okay?"

"Yeah, Just shook up some." She gestured to the spilled groceries. "And now I gotta get more flour. Thanks for steppin' in like you did. That heel would've punched me for sure."

"I wasn't gonna let that happen. Who was he to you?"

Della straightened from where she was picking up the cans on the ground. "That … that's the piker who traded me to Joe to cover his gamblin' debts. A real peach, huh!"

"Dang! Maybe I should let Sheriff Carter know about him. He'll want to keep an eye on the heel if he's stayin' around."

"Go ahead, if you want to. I just want to get out of town as soon as I can. I wouldn't put it past Beau to try to cause more trouble for me."

Jake stayed with Della while she bought more flour, and watched as she pulled the truck away from the curb. Only then, did he walk over to the sheriff's station.

Forty-Six

CAN'T GO INTO TOWN

It had been almost three months now since Ruby picked up Alice alongside the road in Roanoke. That very next day, she had presented Alice with her first notebook, and explained how to use it. "We write down all the ugly things that happened to us. Write out the anger and the pain. Then we burn the pages, and it's gone. After a while, it mostly stays gone too."

Twice now, Ruby had returned to town to get more notebooks, as she and Della often joined Alice in writing sessions. She still thought about leaving the area and moving someplace else where she'd not worry about being recognized, but for now she contented herself with doing what she could to help Alice.

"Della, I think we can get another crate in here, if we brace it with a board. Then it won't slide around." Ruby and Della were loading crates of jams and jellies into the bed of the truck for the trip to town. It was mid-April, time for the farmers' market to open up again. Everybody felt the hard times, so even the little money they could get for their goods was welcome. It wasn't cheap to keep five people in food and shelter, not to mention notebooks.

"There. That'll do it," and Della shut the truck's tailgate with a thud. "Let's get goin'."

Before they could get in the cab, the sound of a car could be heard. A dusty old roadster pulled up at the house, and Jake hopped out. "Mornin', ladies! I was hopin' to catch you 'fore you left for town."

"Why, Jake – I do believe you got yourself some wheels. A little worn, but nice. What brings you out here this early? The sun's barely up." Ruby walked around the roadster, looking it over.

"I just … well," he scratched his head, "I figured I should warn you. You might not want to go into town for a while."

"What are you talkin' about? You know we always try to sell stuff at the farmers' market." Ruby was puzzled.

"Have you heard about what they're callin' the Moonshine Conspiracy down in Franklin County?" Jake leaned against the side of the truck.

251

"Isn't that where a bunch of fellas, deputies and lawyers mostly I think, were caught takin' money to protect some moonshiners? Pa heard somethin' about it last time he was in town."

"Yeah, that's it. Well, the trial is set to begin in about a week, down at the old federal building in Roanoke."

"What's that got to do with us goin' to town?" Della asked, sitting on the edge of the porch.

"That trial's a big deal hereabouts. There's gonna be a whole lot of people in town for it, from Franklin County and farther south, mostly men. You told me about that man at the train station, about how much that upset you. Do you want to chance that again? Seems like it's a real risk."

"Oh!" Ruby sat down next to Della, looking stunned. She gestured at the truck. "But we need to try to sell these things. I don't want to risk it, but … we need … Oh, shoot!" She trailed off.

Lida walked out onto the porch, drying her hands on her apron. "Couldn't help overhearin'. These men … they in town already?"

"Miz Malcolm." Jake nodded his head in greeting. "Yeah, some are. The Lenox Hotel's already half booked up. Just gonna get worse till the trial's over. A real circus."

Lida looked at Ruby. "Too risky. You girls stay here and help your Pa. I'll go to town. Many's a time I went on my own. Won't be any different, I figure."

"Thanks, Ma. I hate for you to have to do that, but …."

"Nonsense! Anythin' to protect you girls, Ruby, anythin'. Jake – thank you for warnin' us. You're a good friend. Let me just collect my coat, and I'll be on my way."

Della followed Lida back into the house, and Jake sat down next to Ruby on the porch. "Look, there's somethin' else I wanted to tell you too. My Ma kept pesterin' me about you, wantin' to know why I wasn't courtin' you."

Ruby laughed. "What did you tell her?"

"I didn't tell her the truth, exactly. I ended up tellin' her that you had been bad hurt by a man a while back. And that you just weren't lookin' for a man in your life like that again."

"True." Ruby shook her head, looking at the ground.

"She figures somebody broke your heart. And that's close enough to the truth, so I guess we can all live with it."

Ruby reached out and squeezed his arm. "Ma's right, Jake. You are a good friend. Thank you – for the warning, and … for everythin'."

Jake nodded at her as he stood and walked toward his car. Halfway there, he stopped and came back. He stood looking down at her. "You're not gonna stay around here, are you?" he asked softly.

Ruby sighed. "Probably not. It's hard on my folks, feedin' all of us. And it's … well, risky, I guess."

"What're you gonna do?"

"Don't know yet. I loved teachin' the little ones, but I'm not sure that's right for me anymore."

"I'm bettin' you could get a teaching job around here now. I hear the schools are gettin' back to normal again."

"It's temptin', except for one thing."

"What's that?"

"How long do you think it would be before the father of one of my students showed up for a conference and remembered my face? Don't forget, it happened at the train station. What's to keep it from happenin' at a school? It'd wreck me for sure."

"It nigh unto killed your folks when you disappeared. I can't imagine they will want to see you leave again."

"I know. If I do decide to go, it won't be far. Then, hopefully, my folks won't feel like their losin' me again."

"So what're you gonna do?" Jake repeated.

"I'm not sure. Della and I have been talkin', but …." She shrugged.

"You've done good work with Alice, y'know."

"Surprised me, but I kinda liked workin' with her. I'd like to keep doin' that, maybe. And I guess it's still teachin', just with bigger folks." She stood. "Don't you need to get on to the hospital, or do they just let you come in when you want?"

"Oh, shoot!" and Jake sprinted for his car.

Forty-Seven

THREATS AND COUNTERTHREATS

May 1935
Roanoke, Virginia

The Moonshine Conspiracy trial was in full swing in Roanoke. Sheriff Atlee set out that morning for the courthouse, hoping to get into the courtroom, even if only for a little while. The subpoena for his testimony at the trial had shaken him, and he wanted to get a feel for what to expect when his turn on the stand came. As he passed a narrow alley near the courthouse building, he thought he heard his name called out.

"Atlee!" came the hiss again. "We need to talk."

Atlee recognized the voice now. "Ray. Never thought I'd see your ugly mug again, 'specially this close to a courthouse." Atlee stepped cautiously into the alley.

"I heard you got subpoenaed for this circus." Ray gestured to the courthouse. "What they want to talk to you about?"

"Dunno. Probably just wanna see if I knew about the payoffs and such. Or if I was part of the mess. All I'm gonna tell 'em is that I heard rumors about somethin' goin' on, but that's it."

Ray glared at him, grabbing a fistful of Atlee's shirt and pulling him close. "That better be all you tell 'em. You so much as breathe a word about our set-up … just you remember you were paid well to look the other way. You turn me in, I'll sing pretty, and you'll go down too."

Atlee knocked Ray's hand away. "I'm not proud of what I did, but at least I never killed nobody."

"What you mean by that?"

"From what I hear, you killed Joe – or as near about as makes no nevermind. And then there's the bodies buried in the woods."

"You can't prove nothin'."

Atlee laughed. "Maybe I can't, but the Malcolm girl sure can. I hear she talked to the law here in Roanoke. Told 'em about you and Joe. Pretty much everythin' too."

"Bitch!" Ray ground out. "Then they know about you too."

"That's the odd thing." Atlee chose his words with care. "For some reason, she didn't say a word about me." If Ray found out how he'd tried to help Ruby, Atlee knew the man would most likely kill him.

"Mebbe she got sweet on you." Ray snorted. "You just remember, you say anythin' about me when you get up on that stand, you gonna take the fall with me."

"And you remember," Atlee poked Ray in the chest, "I know everythin' you did. Everythin'. You turn on me, I'll see you fry for sure."

"I guess we understand each other, then."

"I guess we do."

Forty-Eight

CELINE'S LETTER

June 1935
Roanoke, Virginia

Tom and Lida returned from town, just as supper was almost ready. Della and Alice went out to help unpack the truck, but returned with one small crate only half full.

Tom thumped his hat against his leg as he crossed the threshold. "I gotta say, all the outsiders in town these days can make it hard on a body, but they sure do buy up the jams and jellies you ladies make. We almost sold out."

"One fella even bought that lap blanket Alice made from all the tail ends of yarn we had saved up. Said it was for his wife back home – a piece of 'real hill craft' I think he called it." Lida shook her head. "All the while with a tarted-up woman hangin' off his arm. Some people!"

"That's swell, Ma. His money's as good as anybody's, I guess. Soon as y'all wash up, we can eat, okay?" Ruby stirred the pot of stew on the stove.

"Oh – I almost forgot." Tom dug in his coat pocket. "Ruby, you got a letter here."

"Really? Who from?" She took the letter from him. "It's from Raleigh." She eagerly slit open the letter and sat at the table to read it. "It's from Celine."

"Who?" asked Alice as she set the table around Ruby.

"I told you about her. She's the French gal I got to know at Doris's place. She's good people. You'd like her if you could meet her." Excited, she stood. "Oh … oh … and you're gonna get that chance. She's comin' here to see us." Ruby read some more of the letter. "She says she decided it was finally time for her to move on. And she's got somethin' she wants to talk to me about."

"She say about what?" Lida asked. "I remember you tellin' us about her when you first got home."

"No. Just that she wants to see me and meet you and Pa, and talk."

"Does she say when she's comin'?" Della asked Ruby.

"June thirtieth. She's askin' for someone to meet her train."

"We can do that. It'll be good to meet her, though I feel I already kinda know her, as much as you've talked about her." Tom rubbed his stomach. "That stew 'bout ready? I'm mighty hungry after dealin' with those outsiders today."

Della pulled a tray of biscuits from the oven. "Set yourself on down. What's the news of the big trial?"

While they ate supper, Tom and Lida filled the girls in on what they'd heard in town. "It's been almost ten weeks now since the trial began. Plenty of time to decide who done what, if you ask me. They're sayin' it should be finished up pretty soon," Tom summed up.

"As much as I like the extra money they bring us, I'm lookin' forward to bein' shut of those folks. Some woman stopped your Pa on the street today askin' if he had any 'shine to sell! Can you believe that?"

Ruby laughed. "What'd you tell her, Pa?"

"That she was barkin' up the wrong tree." Tom grinned at her. "She thought that was 'quaint', I think she said."

Alice cleared her throat. "Speakin' of it being time to move on, I have been thinkin' …. I want to try to go see my Ma in Richmond. I'm hopin' she'll want me back, but I guess I won't know until I get there."

"Are you sure about that? You're welcome to stay here a while longer if you need to. I wouldn't want you to leave if you aren't ready." Lida reached out and touched the girl's hand.

"Yeah, I'm sure. Y'all have been real good to me, takin' me in and helpin' me make some sense of what happened to me. But … well, now it's time to go home … to try to go home, at least. When you go to town to get Celine, I'd like to ride along and catch a bus headin' north."

Tom nodded, and the rest of the meal passed in a flurry of advice and well wishes for Alice's trip.

Forty-Nine

RAY'S THREATS

"I wouldn't move too quick if I were you."

Ruby gasped and froze at the feel of the knife against her throat. She dropped the bucket of chicken feed she'd been holding, as cold metal pressed against her neck, an arm roughly yanking her back. "And don't scream neither. I could kill you quicker than anybody could get out here to the barn. You know who this is?"

"Ray," whispered Ruby.

"Good … that's good. I'm mighty angry with you, girl. I hear tell you told the law here in Roanoke that I killed Joe."

"I just told 'em what I saw, him lyin' there dead-like, and the house on fire."

"I heard different."

263

"Well, you heard wrong. Course I did tell Sheriff Carter all about what you and Joe were doin' at the house. He was mighty interested in that."

"I should kill you right now. Slit your throat and be done."

"You could. And that would make four people you murdered, at least four that I know of. And when they find my body, they'll figure it was you done me in. You can be sure the law will hunt you down. And you'll fry."

"They'd have to catch me first." Ray pressed against her. "Maybe I should just take you again, for old time's sake, hmmm? You want that, Gimp?"

"You could try, but I'm not gonna make it easy for you."

Ray laughed and shoved Ruby toward a stack of hay bales. She stumbled forward, grabbed the sickle laying in the shadows atop the hay, and spun, slashing at him. Ray howled as the sharp sickle connected with his arm, gashing it deeply, and causing him to drop his knife. Clutching the wound with his other hand, he backed away. Ruby was startled to see a flash of fear in his eyes.

Ruby raised the sickle and glared at him. "Come at me again, and I'll gut you! You got ten seconds to get out of here. I see you ever again, I'll kill you." Five seconds later, Ruby found herself alone in the dim light of the barn. She sank to the ground, wrapping her arms around herself as she rocked back and forth. After a bit, she stood on shaky legs, picking up the pail of chicken feed. *Well, at least that didn't spill.*

Fifty

CELINE ARRIVES

June 30, 1935
Roanoke, Virginia

After finishing their usual round of morning chores on the farm, Lida and Tom took Alice to the bus station, before picking up Celine when the 2pm train came in.

"Just look for a slender gal, about this high," Ruby had told them, gesturing to indicate Celine was about her height, "and dressed real classy. Blond hair too."

"Shoot – I was just gonna hold up a sign with 'Celine' on it," Tom replied.

Ruby laughed. "That'd work too."

Ruby and Della hurried to finish up their chores in the barn before Ruby's folks would return with Celine in tow. There'd been fox tracks crossing the yard that morning, so they took extra care making sure that the chicken coop was secure, or as secure as you could make it considering how wily foxes were. They were almost back to the house, hoping to have a chance to clean up a bit, when they heard Tom's truck coming up the road.

"Ruby!" Celine squealed, jumping from the truck as it came to a stop. She caught Ruby in a fierce hug, spinning her around.

Ruby hugged her back, laughing. "That pretty dress of yours had better wash up easy. It's got dirt from the barn and the chicken coop on it now!"

Celine looked down at the front of her dress. She brushed off a bit of straw and grinned. "*Oui*, you do smell a bit odd, too. But no matter – it is good to see you again!" and she hugged Ruby again.

The next few hours were spent in lively chatter as the women caught up. Della was introduced to Celine, and they were soon chatting like fast friends.

"Your letter said you wanted to talk to me about something. What is it?" Ruby asked, after a while.

"Oh, that can wait. I am most interested in what you and your parents have done here." Celine turned to Tom. "How many young women have you taken in this past year?"

"Includin' the one gal we took to the bus station a'fore we collected you, it'd be six. They'd stay a bit till they felt able to move on."

"Ruby was right. She told me you had a good heart, and would help those who came in her name." She patted Tom's arm as he blushed at her praise. "Where did they go when they left you?"

"About half said they'd try to go home. The other half we sent on down to Lida's folk in North Carolina."

Lida took up the tale. "My older brother, Hank, had a small dairy farm outside of Hickory, North Carolina. When he passed early last year, keepin' it goin' was real hard on his wife, Eleanor. She needed help, and the girls needed a place to go to, so …. I hear tell it's worked out real fine."

"And it got them away from this area where they might be recognized, *non*?"

"Which reminds me – it looks like the big trial is about to be over. We saw Sheriff Carter in town, and he said the verdict is gonna be handed down tomorrow. Then we get our town back, once all the rubberneckers go home." Tom shook his head.

"What is this trial you talk about?" Celine asked. They had to explain about the Moonshine Conspiracy trial, and how Ruby and Della had been holed-up on the farm for the past ten weeks. "I am impressed. We had heard, even in Raleigh, that there was a big to-do, and some lawmen had been involved. But I guess we didn't realize it might affect you. You did good to stay away from town, I think."

"Being recognized once was bad enough. We didn't want to chance it again," Ruby returned. Celine's confused expression led to an explanation of the day Ruby had found Alice.

"So you introduced her to writing and burning, like you showed me. Is good!" Celine beamed at her. "You still write things down?"

"Sometimes, but not much anymore. I'm not so confused and angry these days. At least usually."

"It is the same for me. Before I left Doris's, I burnt up the rest of my old notebooks. Poof. It was time. And it made quite a lot of fire in the fireplace." Celine grinned at her friend.

Ruby laughed. "I'll just bet it did. I'm proud of you. How's Doris?" she asked, changing the subject.

"She is very good. Something you said to her before you left us got her thinking. She closed the other side of the house, you know."

"What? That's great news. But what about the money it was bringin' in to keep the house goin'?"

"Two new girls came to us who sew like the dream. Doris now runs the most stylish of dress shops in all Raleigh. Very *haute couture*."

"And it brings in enough money?"

"That it does. Even more. You would blush at the prices Doris charges the ladies. This dress here is one of hers, and you got chicken dirt on it."

Ruby laughed. "Sorry 'bout that, but …"

Celine waved her hand, dismissively. "*Non*, is no problem. You are worth it." It was very late that night before they ran out of things to talk about and finally went to bed.

Fifty-One

MOVING ON

July 1935
Roanoke, Virginia

"Walk with me. Show me this wonderful coop of your chickens."

Sweaters draped over their shoulders, Celine and Ruby walked the short distance to the chicken coop, nestled up beside the barn. Ruby explained to her friend how the coop was set up, and introduced Celine to her favorite chickens. "That one there? I named her Doris 'cause she kinda runs the coop."

"Hmmm." Celine cocked her head, considering the chicken in question. "I'm not sure I see that it looks like our friend, Doris, but I will take your word for it." She turned to look at Ruby. "So tell me, please, what is it you want to do with your life now that you have it back again?"

"I've been thinkin' about that a lot lately. It has been real good to be home these past months, but

271

I know I can't stay here forever. What kinda life would it be if I had to hide out up here and be afraid to go into town 'cause of who I might run into?" Ruby grimaced and shook her head.

"That is problem for many who go home."

Ruby rubbed her shoe back and forth in the dirt. "I want to do somethin' that counts … that's worth somethin'. Do some good. Not just to make up for what I had to do at Joe's, but … well, because I can. And should."

"So what would it be that is worth something to you?"

"I think I'd like to do somethin' like what Doris does, like what my folks are doin' – but just not here. I've been thinkin' about goin' to my Aunt Eleanor's. You remember the dairy farm outside of Hickory that Ma told you about?" At Celine's nod, she continued. "If I settled in there, and worked hard at it, maybe I could set up another safe place, a place where girls and women who've been hurt could heal. Like what Doris did for us. It'd take time, it'd be hard, but I think I could do it."

"*Oui*, you can do it. But you don't have to do it alone. I will help."

"What do you mean?"

"I do not plan to go back to Raleigh. Doris taught me well how to keep the books, and you too taught me much. It is time for me to start fresh, like you. So I go with you to this Hickory, and we can name a cow there after Doris. Just don't tell her!"

"Havin' you with me would be a blessin', but have you ever been around cows before?"

Celine waved her hand dismissively and grinned. "Is no problem. You teach me. Instead of chicken dirt, my clothes will have cow dirt on them. Or maybe I help your aunt manage things and you can go play with the cows. We ask Della, too, *oui*?"

Ruby nodded. "I'm bettin' she'll want to come with us. Let's go ask her. And I'd better write Aunt Eleanor to ask if she'll have us." Arm in arm, Ruby and Celine wandered back to the house.

Fifty-Two

IN THE BLACK

June 1938
Hickory, North Carolina

It had been three years since Ruby, Della, and Celine got off the bus in Hickory, North Carolina. A lot had happened in those three years.

Celine finished her last entry, and closed the dairy's ledger with a snap. She stood and stretched, walking to the window to look out. She watched Ruby and Della come out of the barn and head across the yard. From the expression on their faces, she could tell they had good news.

"Celine," Ruby called out as she entered the house, "Doris just dropped a fine little calf. She did great!"

Celine laughed. "That is great news. Next time you write Doris in Raleigh, you should tell her about this cow named for her. First a chicken, now a cow.

She will get the laugh out of it, *oui*? Now you go get cleaned up. I start supper."

"Deal. Martha and Norma are finishin' up the evenin' milking. Should be in soon."

An hour later, there was much to celebrate as the five women gathered around the table for supper. The new calf, dubbed Daisy Mae by Della, was healthy and doing well. And, if that wasn't enough to celebrate, Celine shared her news.

"So when I do the books today, I find we are again in the black ink. It is six months now that we do that. Ladies," she raised her water glass in salute, "we are a success!"

Amid the cheers and excited conversation that followed Celine's announcement, Ruby thought back to when she, Celine, and Della had first arrived at her aunt's farm. There had been five cows, only four of which could be milked, and the farm had been just barely able to make ends meet, let alone show a profit. A year later, Aunt Eleanor sold the place to the three girls, lock, stock, and barrel, moving into town to be closer to friends. Though the property was registered in all their names equally, it had been Celine's money from her late husband's estate that secured the property for them. When Celine was staying with Doris, a lawyer friend of hers had managed to safeguard the estate until she needed the funds.

"He was a wicked man, but we can use his money for the good start for us," she had insisted. "It is least he can do. Fitting, *oui*?" When Ruby and Della had argued against putting the farm in all their names, Celine held firm. "We are a team. It will make us work harder, if I do this."

It had been hard, too. Only Ruby had any real experience working with dairy cows, though Della at least knew which end of the cow to milk. Eleanor patiently taught them what they needed to know, sharing with them her love of the farm and the life.

"It scared me when Hank and I started this place twenty some years ago. The cows were so big and smelly." Eleanor laughed. "Then the first calf was born, and … well, I came to love it. If Hank hadn't passed …." She shook her head, "It's too much for me now, but you girls, you can make it work."

And she had been right. It didn't take long for them to come to love the dairy as Eleanor had. It also didn't take long for them to realize that Celine was better suited to keeping the books than milking the cows. The day she punched a cow for knocking over a full pail of milk was the day Ruby relieved her of working with the animals. It was now two years since that incident, and they had turned things around. They now had ten cows, and sold their milk, butter and cheeses in town, making a small profit.

Martha showed up, almost a year and a half after they'd arrived in Hickory. She came to them from Raleigh, having spent some time with Doris after escaping from an abusive marriage. Martha had been raised on a farm, and she fit right into the daily life on the dairy. She didn't talk much about what she'd escaped, but every couple of weeks she'd have a nightmare. Ruby would fix her a big mug of warm vanilla milk, and sit up with her when it happened. Sometimes they'd talk, and sometimes they'd just sit in silence.

Norma turned up during a thunderstorm one night, drenched and cranky. At first, Ruby thought the crankiness was just from trudging through the storm, but she soon realized that Norma was almost always surly. Ruby figured it was just Norma's way of keeping people at a distance. She explained that after losing her job, she'd ended up on the streets, where she was snatched up and forced into prostitution. Surprisingly, Norma and Martha quickly became close. Norma was a city-slicker, and Martha had her work cut out for her, getting the woman up to speed at the dairy. While Norma never punched a cow like Celine did, she was prone to cursing at them upon occasion.

Ruby still kept a journal, writing and burning bits of her past, but she did that less and less. The hard work of the dairy consumed most of her time, leaving her little time for writing and introspection. Every new girl who came to the farm was given a notebook and encouraged to write things out. Some took to it, and others didn't.

While Ruby missed her parents and Jake, they managed to keep in touch with letters. Every couple of weeks, a letter would arrive, full of the goings-on at either the veterans' hospital or the Malcolm's farm.

"Ruby, you got another letter from Jake," Della called out, waving the envelope as she entered the kitchen.

"That's two this month. I wonder what's new." Ruby wiped her hands on her apron and took the letter from Della. They settled at the kitchen table, as Ruby slit open the envelope with the knife she'd been using to chop onions. "That's swell! He's heard from Wilhelm Dietrich. You remember him, don't you, Della? He's that veteran Jake brought out for Sunday dinner, the one who was goin' up to Asheville." Eyes on the letter in her hand, Ruby failed to notice Della's blush.

"What'd he hear?"

278

"That Will's doin' much better up in Asheville. Oteen was a good place to send him. He's got himself a job workin' at the Biltmore Estate as a gardener, too."

Della smiled. "I'm glad to hear that. He was an interesting man. Did you know he played piano? Jake told me he was pretty good, too."

"Didn't know that. You warmin' to him?"

"Maybe. Don't know. He's just … interestin'." Della stood. "Come on. Dinner isn't gonna make itself."

Fifty-Three

CLARA AND DANNY

June 1938
Hickory, North Carolina

Ruby crossed the yard, carrying a crate full of tubs of butter destined for the farmers' co-op in town. As she neared the house, she spotted a man and a woman walking up the farm's long dirt drive. Setting the crate inside the kitchen door, she returned to the yard to greet the couple.

"Afternoon," she called out. As they neared her, she couldn't help but notice that the woman was very pregnant. "You all right, ma'am?"

"Just real tired." The woman pressed her hands against her lower back. "Woman in town named Eleanor said you might help us out. We just need a place to stay till the baby's born. We can work for our keep. My brother, Danny, is kinda simple, but he's strong. And I could cook and clean for you."

"What did Eleanor tell you about us?"

"Not much. She said that the women here had reasons not to trust men, but that it wouldn't hurt to ask if we could stay for a bit."

"That's true. We don't have many men visitors. We don't hate men as a whole, but … well, Eleanor was right to say some here have good reasons not to trust men."

"My feelings exactly. This," The woman rubbed her belly, "this wasn't my idea. My Pa … Danny and I had to get out of there." She reached back and took Danny's hand, while he continued to hang his head and look at the ground.

"I'm inclined to say y'all can stay for a couple of months, but I'm gonna have to ask the rest of the ladies if it's okay with them. Why don't you come on in and sit a spell? Stay for supper. You can tell us your story, and ask the ladies if y'all can stay."

"We'd be mighty grateful! We haven't had a good meal in ages. I'm about done in, and Danny … well, new things confuse him, and he gets real quiet. My name's Clara, by the way." The pair followed Ruby toward the house.

"I'm Ruby. That was my Aunt Eleanor you met in town." Ruby got them settled at the kitchen table with cups of coffee. "Put your feet up, Clara. Y'all can keep me company while I make supper."

About then, Della clattered down the stairs and into the kitchen, stopping short when she saw Danny. "Oh! You still want me to take the butter into town, Ruby?"

"Yeah. You've just got time to get in and back 'fore supper. We'll be fine here."

Della deftly caught the keys Ruby tossed her. She grabbed a cardigan off the back of a kitchen chair and picked up the crate by the door. "Be right back, then."

As Ruby set about making a potatoes and ham casserole, she talked with Clara and Danny about the dairy. "There's five of us here now, makin' it work. We all come from ... well, let's just say we all know what it's like to be mistreated by men. Sorry, Danny, but they may not want you to stay here."

"It's okay. I'm Danny." He gave Ruby a wide child-like smile, before returning his attention to the potato he was meticulously peeling.

Over supper that evening, with everybody gathered around the table, Clara asked the group if she and Danny could stay. "At least till the baby's born. And that's not far off, I'm thinking," she said, rubbing her belly. "Don't know what we'll do if we have to go."

"What're y'all runnin' from?" Martha asked. "That's why you're on the road, isn't it?"

Clara nodded. "It is. Up until about three months ago, we were living with our Pa on a small farm over in Kentucky, near Louisville. Once Ma died, Pa kinda snapped. He got real mean. He'd beat Danny when Danny didn't understand something. And he … he decided I should take Ma's place in his bed." She shuddered.

"But that's just wrong!" Martha called out in shock.

"You got that right! I was too afraid of what he'd do to Danny if I ran off, so I had to stay." She patted Danny's hand. "And the babe? It's his. As mean as he'd got, I was afraid he'd kill it the first time it cried. So one day, when he was in town, we ran. Been hiding out mostly, and working when we could."

"You think he'll come this way lookin' for you?" Della frowned at her. "Or get the law involved?"

"Not likely. Kentucky's far enough away. If he had the law looking for me, he'd have to explain the babe. I don't think his little church would understand, do you? By now, the church ladies will have taken him to heart. I'll bet anything he's fixin' to marry Widow Matthews. Good luck to her!"

"*Oui*. Good luck to her." Celine nodded toward Danny. "But what about Danny? As you say, he is simple. But he is a man nonetheless, *non*?"

"He has always been like this, a sweet little boy. We didn't really notice at first. But when he got to be three or four, we knew something was off. Now …" she shrugged, "now he's still a sweet simple little boy."

Norma snorted. "But in a man's body. Has he shown any interest in girls? That's my concern here."

"He has not. Look, I understand your worries. If it's too much to ask, we'll keep on going. We have to stay together. If he's not welcome to stay, then we both have to leave. I can't abandon him – I'm all he's got. Could we at least spend the night in the barn and leave in the morning? I'm sorry, but I couldn't walk another step tonight."

Norma shook her head. "No, Clara. I'm the one who's sorry. I gather Ruby told you we all have reasons not to trust men. It makes us real cautious."

Della spoke up. "Let's put it to a vote. Seems to me that we've got three choices here. One, that we send Clara and Danny packing in the mornin'. Two, that we let them both stay, but out in the barn. We can fix up the tack room out there so's it would be fine. And three, that we let them both stay, and Danny bunks out in the barn, and Clara's in here with us."

"I agree – let's vote on it." Ruby looked around the table. "Who's in favor of sending Danny and Clara away in the mornin'?" No hands were raised. "Okay. So who's in favor of them both bunkin' in the barn?" Again, no hands were raised. "Does that mean you all agree to let them stay, her in here, him in the barn?"

"Yeah. With the understandin' that he behaves himself. I know how to use the pointy end of a pitchfork to defend myself. And I would, too." Martha tapped on the table for emphasis.

"You won't regret this, I promise." Clara had tears in her eyes.

Ruby stood. "It's decided then. Clara, I'll bet you could use a long hot bath to soak some of the aches out of your muscles. And then bed. Norma and Celine, would you see to that?" At their nods, she continued. "Martha, Della and I will show Danny where he can bunk down in the barn. Oh," she paused, looking at Clara, "will he come with me and do what I tell him?"

"Sure, but let me explain things to him again so he doesn't get scared. He'll like being near the animals anyway." The women cleared the table, while Clara explained things to Danny. As Clara had predicted, Danny was thrilled that he got to sleep with the cows.

"No accountin' for taste," Martha muttered as they walked Danny out to the barn. Della and Ruby showed him the bunk in the tack room, while Martha rounded up some spare blankets and a pillow. They left him with a big flashlight, promising to introduce him to all the cows in the morning.

Ruby smiled at him. "They need their beauty sleep, so you leave them alone for now. Promise?"

"I promise!"

"Come up to the house at sunup for breakfast, okay?" Della turned to leave. "Goodnight."

"Goodnight, Ladies!" Danny grinned at them and hummed a few bars of the tune. As they left the barn, they heard him call out, "Goodnight, pretty cows."

Fifty-Four

GRACIE

August 1938
Hickory, North Carolina

"It's time!" Martha shook Ruby awake. "Ruby, the baby's coming. Wake up!"

"I'm comin', I'm comin'." Ruby grabbed her robe off the hook and followed Martha down the hallway to Clara's room. It was there, at 3AM, that little Grace was born. Ruby thanked her lucky stars that Martha had some training as a midwife.

"A mite small," observed Della later at breakfast, "but, considerin' what all Clara's been through, not bad. Good set of lungs, though."

"Cute, too." Martha smiled.

Norma raised an eyebrow and just looked at her. "Aren't you sweet! She's still all red and puckered up from bein' born. She'll be cute in a day or two."

Ruby was concerned about Clara. The birth had, mercifully, not been difficult, but when Grace was placed in Clara's arms, the young woman simply sat and stared at the little baby. Luckily, Martha, coming from a large family, was used to caring for infants. She knew what needed to be done, and helped Clara start nursing Grace. Still, Ruby couldn't help but think that Clara was too quiet, too subdued.

Over the next five months, Clara seemed to adjust to being a new mother, cuddling the baby, singing her nonsense songs made up on the fly. The baby was thriving, spoiled by all the attention showered on her by her five 'aunties'. Danny took to Grace from the start, insisting she had to be introduced to all the cows. After supper, he would sit on the porch with Grace, telling her about the antics of the cows that day. He was very proud to be an uncle, and took to introducing himself as 'Uncle Danny'.

One morning, Ruby woke to hear Grace crying. Not an unusual occurrence, but when Clara didn't quiet her, and the crying kept up, Ruby went to check on the baby. She found her in the wooden crate that was her bed. The baby was flailing her arms and legs, sobbing, her face all red and scrunched up. There was no sign of Clara. Her bed showed no sign of having been slept in, and there was a folded piece of paper with Ruby's name on it, propped up against the pillow.

Della staggered into the room, rubbing sleep from her eyes. "What's goin' on?"

"Don't know yet, but I'm figurin' it's not good." Ruby picked up the baby, handing her to Della. "Here, you see if you can calm her down, while I read Clara's note."

"Uh oh." Della rubbed Grace's back, humming to her.

"Yeah." Ruby picked up Clara's note, sitting down on the side of the bed to read it.

> *Dear Ruby,*
>
> *I can't do this. I've tried to love Grace, tried to do right by her, but every time I look at her, I remember who her Pa is. I can't get past it. I know it's not her fault, but I just can't hold her without remembering what he did to me.*
>
> *I know you must think me a horrible person. You must hate me. I can understand that. I'm just too weak. Please take care of Grace. Find her a good home. Danny and I will head out west and try our luck there.*
> *Clara*

Ruby read the note out loud to Della. "I can't say I'm surprised."

"Me neither. Not sure what I'd do in her situation, but I'd like to think I'd not be leavin' my baby behind. What do we do now?" Della had managed to calm Grace a bit, but she was still fussing.

"Guess we should heat up some milk and see if she'll take it. We can be figurin' out the rest later."

When the five women gathered for breakfast that morning, they discussed what to do about Grace. Norma was of the opinion that they should contact the local sheriff. Ruby nixed the idea immediately. "If the sheriff managed to trace Clara and Danny ... maybe their Pa told the law in Kentucky they'd run off. Pretty sure he'd have to send Grace to their Pa since he's family. Do we want that?"

Amid a chorus of No's, Ruby sat in the rocker in the corner of the kitchen and began to rock the baby.

"Can't we just keep her?" Martha laughed. "I know she's not exactly a puppy that showed up on the doorstep, but couldn't we just raise her ourselves?"

"I'd like to do that, but ... well, it could get complicated. Won't we need some kinda legal paperwork and all? To make it look like a proper adoption so they can't take her away from us. And

she might need a birth certificate sooner or later …
maybe for when she goes to school." Ruby frowned.
"We can't afford a lawyer, even if we could find one
who'd be willin' to gloss over how we came by
Grace."

"What if one of us went away for a few days,
and came back with her? We could say we adopted
her somewhere else," Della offered.

"We'd still need legal papers eventually, I'm
guessin'.

"*Oui*, we would." Celine nodded thoughtfully.
"I think I can help with that. You remember my
lawyer friend, back in New Orleans? The one who
helped me get the money to buy this farm? She is a
survivor, like we all are. I am very sure she would help
us keep our little Grace with us. She will know what
papers we need. I will write her today and ask, if you
agree."

"Bless your heart, Celine. If she could do that
for us, it'd be a blessing for sure." Ruby stood,
placing the sleeping baby in a padded laundry basket.
"Meantime, we have some cows that need milkin'."
As Celine got out stationary and settled at the kitchen
table to write her letter, Ruby led the others outside to
begin their daily routine.

Fifty-Five

BETTY

January 1939
Hickory, North Carolina

"Ruby," Della let the kitchen curtain fall back into place, "the sheriff just pulled up out front."

"Let me go see what he wants. Martha, why don't you take Gracie upstairs for now." Ruby stepped out onto the porch. "Mornin', Sheriff. Don't see you out this way much. What can I do for you?"

"Mornin', Miss Ruby. Your Aunt Eleanor said I should come see you." He motioned at his car, and a young girl, maybe thirteen or so, stepped out hesitantly. Her cheek was bruised, one eye starting to swell shut, her lip split.

"Oh, my! What happened?"

"Betty's Pa took issue with her tone of voice. Thought he'd smack some respect into her. Eleanor said you'd likely take the girl in, least till her Pa sobers up and things settle down."

292

"Of course, we will." Ruby crossed over to Betty. "You're safe here, honey. Come on inside." At the door, she turned back to the sheriff. "Thanks, Sheriff. Thanks for bringing her here. I'd invite you in for coffee, but we're in the middle of a real early spring cleaning, and things are all topsy-turvy." He tipped his hat to them, got back in the car, and drove off.

Ruby sat Betty down at the kitchen table and inspected the damage to her face. "Hmmm. I have some salve that'll help with this. Let me go get it."

Betty looked around the kitchen in confusion. "You lied to the sheriff. Why?"

"Whatever do you mean?" Ruby paused at the hallway door.

"You told him you were in the middle of cleaning, and you're not."

"Oh that. Betty, we have as little as we can to do with menfolk. Him bein' a lawman … doesn't matter. We'd rather keep men out of here." She gestured around the room.

Della hung up the dishtowel, finished with the dishes. "Ruby, you go get that salve. I'll fill Betty in." She sat down at the table across from the girl. By the time Ruby returned, Martha and Gracie in tow, Della had given Betty a broad picture of their history. "Ah, now you get to meet the other reason we didn't want the sheriff in here. Betty, meet Gracie."

"She's adorable! Why is she a secret?" Betty wanted to know.

"You can't tell a soul she's here. Promise!" Martha hugged the baby.

"Okay, I won't say nothin'. But why?"

Ruby gently rubbed some of the salve she was holding on Betty's bruised cheek. "Her mom left her with us, and we're workin' on adoptin' her, legal-wise. Sheriff'd feel obliged to return her to … well, to a really bad man."

"Is he her Pa?" At Ruby's nod, Betty continued. "Then doesn't she belong with him? What'd he do that's so bad?"

Della slapped the table hard, causing Gracie to startle and cry. "He beat his son and fucked his daughter, that's what he did. No way does he get his hands on this little girl!"

"Oh!" Betty paled, and looked down at her hands clasped in her lap. "You're right, no way can he have her." She spoke in almost a whisper. "Can I hold her?"

Gracie quieted right away, once she was in Betty's arms. Ruby sat down next to the girl. She put her forefinger under Betty's chin and lifted until the girl was looking her in the eyes. "You want to tell us what happened? Has your Pa been messin' with you?"

Betty swallowed hard. "Just beatin' me so far. The few times he's tried to touch me like you mean, I was able to stall him till he passed out drunk."

"So far," Martha commented.

"Yeah, so far. I don't want to go back home, but I'm guessin' I'll have to. I don't know what else to do."

Ruby looked at the others. "We'll think on it some. Meantime, you take Gracie and go sit in the rocker there. You can feed her a bottle. Do you both good to rock a spell."

Over the next three weeks, Betty settled into life at the dairy farm. She even learned to milk a cow, which was an experience for her.

"You want me to grab what?"

"Her teats. And don't grab. Wrap your thumb and forefinger around it, like so. Here, let me show

295

you. Like that. Now you try it." Ruby stood so Betty could sit on the low stool.

After a few false starts, she managed to coax a spurt of milk out of the patient cow. "Well, if that don't beat all! I did it!" Betty beamed, smiling ear-to-ear. "Now, maybe I can earn my keep." She looked up at Ruby anxiously. "You're not gonna send me back, are you?"

"Not if you don't want to go. I talked about it with the others, and they agree. You can stay here with us, or we can help you get someplace else. Your choice. Now let's finish up with the milkin'. It'll be supper time soon."

Ruby finished up with the last of the cows, settling them into the barn for the night, when they heard a truck rattle into the yard. A truck door slammed.

"Betty, I know you're in there. Get out here now," a man bellowed.

"Oh, no!" It's my Pa." Betty grabbed Ruby's arm. "You can't send me back, you just can't. Please." Even in the dim light of the barn, Ruby could see the frantic look in Betty's eyes.

"Don't you worry none." Ruby pointed to the shotgun hanging on the wall by the barn door. "Knew there was a reason I kept this here. If I send you back for it, you move quick, okay? Come on. Time for you to face down your devil." Ruby and Betty left the barn, stopping a few feet from it.

"There you are. Get in the truck, girl. I'm takin' you home." The man staggered to a stop in front of them, shaking his fist. He was unkempt, and the smell of cheap booze rolled off him in waves.

"You got no business here. Betty's told me how you've been treatin' her. I despise a mean ol' bully, hurtin' someone you should be protectin'."

"The girl's been lyin' to you. I never done nothin' a daddy shouldn't do to raise up a kid right."

"You're a drunk old fool if you think beatin' is the right way to raise a kid. Betty's gonna stay with me now, so you can't smack her around none. And right now, you need to get back in your truck and leave."

"You gonna make me, girlie? I don't think so." The man reached out to grab Ruby.

Ruby grabbed his outstretched arm, twisted it behind his back, and spun him around. She pushed him back to his battered old truck, yanked open the door with her free hand, and shoved him inside, slamming the door.

"You can't keep me from my kid. I'll set the sheriff on you, I will." He tried to open the door, but Ruby leaned against it, keeping it closed.

"So you're not just a mean drunk ol' fool, but you're stupid to boot? The sheriff knows all about how you treat this girl. Who do you think brought her out here? Now get out of here and stay gone!" Ruby slapped the side of the old truck and stepped back.

Blinking blearily, the man leaned out the truck's window. "Ah, come on. Betty, baby girl, you wanna come home with your ol' Pa, don't you? Come on." His tone wheedling, the man gestured for her to come.

"No!"

"What you mean by that? Who's gonna take care of me? You get in this truck right now!" The man glared at her.

"No! I'm stayin' here. I'm not goin' with you." Betty was adamant.

"Why you little …."

"That's enough!" Ruby yelled. "Turn this truck around and get out of here. Now!"

Cursing loudly, the man fumbled to start up his truck. "I'm gettin' the sheriff," he bellowed, tires spurting gravel as he wheeled out of the yard.

"Into the house, now," Ruby said gesturing with her chin. She stood in the yard, watching, until the truck was a tiny speck on the horizon. When she came into the house, she found Betty huddled in the kitchen rocker, tears on her face.

"See, we didn't need the shotgun after all." Ruby smiled and handed Betty her handkerchief.

"He'll be back, you know." Betty snuffled.

"Well, you won't be here. We need to talk to the others and make some plans."

Over a simple supper of tomato soup and grilled cheese sandwiches, the group talked about what to do. "Ruby is right. You must not be here when that man returns, with the sheriff or not. We must get you away from here, *non*?" Celine turned to Ruby. "You could take the truck and take her to the bus stop in Hickory. Send her to your parents."

"I don't want her riding the bus by herself. It's too dangerous."

"*Oui*, that it is. So what else …"

Norma stood, scooped a set of keys out of a kitchen drawer, and handed them to a startled Ruby. "I have a better plan," she said. "Take my old jalopy. She ain't pretty, but she works. You take Betty to your folks. Take Gracie with you, and then when the paperwork is all final, you can come back. We can handle things here. And we can handle the sheriff, if need be. We'll tell him you left to go visit your folks, and once you were gone, Betty spooked and ran off."

Ruby stared at Norma in surprise. Normally taciturn, this was the most the woman had spoken at one time in a long while. "I'm thinkin' that just might work. Anybody see flaws in Norma's plan?" When there was no response, Ruby continued. "We'll need to leave first thing in the mornin', 'fore Betty's Pa and the sheriff can come back. Martha, you pack up Gracie's things. Della, make up some bottles for her. Celine, can you find a change of clothes for Betty to take?" As they all dispersed to their various tasks, Ruby turned back. "Norma? Thank you."

"It's nothin' you wouldn't do for me. Now go pack a suitcase for yourself. I'll bring the car around so it's ready in the mornin'."

Before the sun was up, as the sky in the east began to lighten, Ruby steered Norma's old jalopy out of the farm yard. There was a hamper full of food on the seat beside her. In the back seat, under a blanket lay Betty and Gracie, a precaution if someone saw them on the road before they could get a few miles away. *I wonder what Ma and Pa will make of Gracie? They're gonna spoil her for sure. It will be good to spend a little time with them again.* As she drove off, away from the dairy that had become her home, Ruby thought about how different returning to Roanoke would be from the last time.

·

Fifty-Six

PEACE

February 1939
Roanoke, Virginia

They'd been on the road for about an hour, before Ruby felt safe to pull over onto the verge. "Y'all can come up front now, if you want. There's nobody followin' us." In short order, Betty was sitting next to Ruby, a sleeping Gracie on her lap. "Sorry you had to hide out like that, but I didn't want to chance somebody seein' you."

"That's okay. It was warm under the blanket, and I fell asleep. How long till we get to your folks' place?" Betty spoke softly so as not to awaken the baby.

"Well, it's around two hundred miles from the dairy to my folks, so I reckon we'll get there by early afternoon. Maybe sooner, but I'm not countin' on that. There may be some snow on the roads that'll slow us down."

"I can spell you some on the drivin' if you want."

"You can drive?" Ruby looked at Betty in surprise.

"Yeah. My Pa taught me to drive his ol' truck last summer. A car can't be that much different."

"I'll keep that in mind. Let's just see how it goes."

They pulled into the yard in front of the Malcolm's farm near Roanoke about mid-afternoon. Along the way, they had stopped only to gas up, stretch a little, and gobble down some of the food they'd brought along. Ruby even let Betty drive a couple of times. They arrived, tired and hungry, glad that the trip was over. They sat for a little bit, listening to the car's engine tick as it cooled down, before they got out of the car. They made it halfway across the yard before the door was thrown open. Lida was down the steps and across the yard in a flash.

"Ruby! Lordy, girl – you sure surprised us. Is everythin' okay?" Lida hugged her daughter fiercely.

"Everythin's okay now," Ruby answered, smiling. "We're so tired we can't see straight, and hungry to boot, but we made it fine."

303

"Who's this with you?" Lida looked at Betty, puzzled.

Juggling the baby on her hip, Betty smiled shyly. "Afternoon, ma'am. I'm Betty, and this here's Gracie."

"Well, I'll be! I know there's a long complicated story here, but you ladies look all done in. Now inside with you. Pa can get your things out of the car when he comes in to supper. Except the baby's – we'll be needin' that, I reckon."

Ruby remembered eating a slab of bread and butter, washing it down with some cold milk, and then not much else until she woke, several hours later. She lay there, wondering what had awoken her, when she heard it again – the sound of the dinner bell on the front porch as Lida rang it to let Tom know supper was about ready.

"I had to get Betty out of there before her Pa came back. No way would I let him get his hands on her again." Ruby was explaining their hasty departure from the dairy farm.

"I wouldn't have gone back with him. I'd have run away." Betty's voice quavered.

"I know. I couldn't abide the idea of you out there on your own. And that's why we're here."

They were sitting around the table after supper, Ruby explaining to her folks why they had arrived out of the blue like they had.

"Betty, you're most welcome here. Don't get your feathers ruffled though if I slip and call you 'Betty Lou' sometimes. I have a cousin by that name. Haven't seen her in ages, but you kinda look like her." Tom grinned at the girl. "Now, tell us about this little lady," he continued as he bounced Gracie on his knees. Your last letter said how you came by her, her mother leavin' her and all. Your Ma said you mentioned an adoption, but she didn't know more."

After Ruby explained her plans for Gracie, Lida still had a question. "But you're not married. Will a judge even let you adopt her, bein' a single woman and all?"

"Celine's lawyer friend is workin' on that. It may take a few months – I don't know. Meantime, we need to stay here till the paperwork's done, and then I can bring Gracie back to the dairy. By the way, Della says she's finally perfected her rhubarb jam recipe, and she sent us with some for you to try."

"I'll be the judge of that," Tom responded, laughing.

Ruby had just dumped a pail of slop into the pig's trough, and stood by the fence watching as the pig noisily ate. "Pa, that is one fat pig!"

"Yeah. It bein' just us, we couldn't keep up with all the milk the cow gave. We put it to good use, fattenin' up the pig. I reckon there'll be lots of good bacon and ham soon." Tom dumped another pail of slop into the trough and came to stand by Ruby. He gently squeezed her shoulder. "You seem different, girl. You finally seem ... at peace, I guess. It's good to see."

Ruby thought about it before she answered. "I guess you're right. I do feel at peace. I can't change what happened to me – if I had my druthers, it wouldn't have happened at all. But to keep railin' at it, to keep lettin' it eat me up inside ...." She shook her head. "I feel like I was able to climb out of that dark place, Pa. Some of the others ... they can't. I was lucky."

"You ever manage to forgive that Ray fella?"

Ruby snorted. "Not sure if it's forgiveness or not, my bein' at peace with everythin'. At least I don't wish him dead anymore, and that's sayin' somethin'."

"That it is. Now enough of this lollygaggin'. We gotta repair that back wall of the smokehouse 'fore we can butcher that pig and start smokin' up some hams." Ruby, Betty, and Gracie had been at the farm near Roanoke for almost three months now, and Ruby had come to treasure the time she spent with her Pa. They'd quickly settled back into their old rhythm of work. The coming of spring meant more work on the farm, and Ruby was glad she was there to help out. While they worked, they talked about many different things, from politics and religion, to farming and hunting. Ruby had always been impressed with the depth of her father's knowledge, and now it was no different. He may not have finished high school, but Tom Malcolm was a very wise man.

Jake resumed his habit of coming out to the farm for the occasional Sunday dinner, and he and Ruby again picked up their friendship where they left off. He laughed at her stories of dealing with recalcitrant cows, and she laughed at his stories of dealing with recalcitrant patients. Betty thought Jake hung the moon, and never missed a chance to bring him coffee, or just sit and listen raptly to his stories.

"You've got a fan there," Ruby teased him as she walked him out to his old car.

Jake groaned and grinned at her. "All us handsome, eligible young doctors have to put up with the attentions of the fairer sex. It's such a burden."

Ruby exploded in laughter. "Oh, Jake … you're so goofy!"

"Seriously, though – Betty'll figure out soon enough she's too young for me, and that I'd make a good older brother. I'm sorry she's been through so much already at her tender age. What's wrong with people, Ruby, that they hurt those they're supposed to take care of? It galls me that I can't fix that problem."

"We both are doin' what we can to heal broken people, Jake. All we can do is keep tryin', I guess. Now you drive careful gettin' home." Ruby stood in the yard, watching until the taillights on Jake's car disappeared around the bend in the road. *He has such a good heart*, she thought as she turned to enter the house.

Fifty-Seven

A RECKONING

March 1939
Roanoke, Virginia

Ruby dropped Betty outside the public library, telling the girl she'd be back to pick her up in about half an hour. "I've got a couple of things to get for Ma at the Piggly Wiggly, and then I'll pick up the mail. Maybe there's word from Celine. You be okay? What're you laughin' at?"

Betty tried to stop giggling, but with little success. "Sorry. The name of the grocery, 'Piggly Wiggly' – it just makes me laugh."

"I know – it's a silly name, but a good store anyway. You gonna be okay on your own?" Ruby asked again.

"Sure. I'll just wait for you on the steps here." With that, Betty bounded up the steps and into the library.

It took Ruby longer than she'd thought to finish her errands. She'd have been on time, but she ran into Jake's Ma in the post office, and, of course, she wanted to gossip and catch up. It was closer to an hour before Ruby turned the corner and parked the truck two cars down from the library. There was no sign of Betty on the steps. Deciding the girl must have decided to wait inside, Ruby slid out of the truck and started down the sidewalk. Then she saw her. Clutching a book to her chest and shaking her head, Betty tried to step back, but a man had a hold on her arm. With his free hand, he was gesturing toward the car parked at the curb. With a jolt, Ruby recognized Ray.

"C'mon, I'll take you home. You don't wanna wait out here," Ruby heard him say as she ran near.

"Let her go, Ray!" Ruby yelled. "You're not gonna hurt another girl."

"Now Ruby, you need to be steppin' back." Ray grinned at her. "Maybe I should tell this young lady 'bout how come you and I know each other. You want that?" Still holding on to Betty's arm, he turned to face Ruby, pulling a gun from his pocket with his free hand.

"Ray, let her go." Ruby repeated. "There's no call to be hurtin' her."

He tipped his head to the side as if he was considering what she'd said. "No, I don't think so. She's coming with me. I'm startin' up my ol' business now, and she'll do just fine."

"No!" Betty screamed. She flung her book at Ray, and began trying to pry his hand off her arm.

As Ray's attention shifted to Betty, Ruby lunged at him. She yanked Betty away, and grabbed for his hand holding the pistol. "Run, Betty, run!" Get help!"

Ruby and Ray wrestled for control of the weapon, both desperately trying to keep the gun pointed away from themselves. Ray tripped her, and they fell heavily to the ground. As they grappled on the sidewalk, suddenly there was a loud BANG. Ray jerked, and then fell limply on top of Ruby. She shoved vainly at Ray's body, becoming aware of voices.

"Are you okay, Miss?" one man asked.

"Here, let me help you up," another said.

"You poor thing! We called for the sheriff," a woman cried out. The small crowd that gathered, pushed Ray's body aside and helped Ruby up. They sat her on the library steps, and someone gave her his sweater to keep warm as she was starting to shake in shock. It also covered up Ray's blood that had soaked into her shirt.

Betty threw herself down next to Ruby. "It's okay," she whispered. "It's okay, it's okay." She held on as Ruby put her head on the girl's shoulder and shuddered.

An hour later, Ruby and Betty sat in the sheriff's office, relating what had happened. "Sheriff Carter, I had to try to stop him from takin' Betty. And then we wrestled for the gun and it went off and …." Tears began rolling down her cheeks again.

"Ruby, you're not in trouble here. By all accounts, you were defendin' Betty and yourself. Considerin' what you've told me about that man, I can't say I'm sorry he's gone."

"So why do I feel so bad? He was as mean as a snake, and an evil excuse for a human being. So why can't I stop shakin' and cryin'?"

"It's the shock of the whole thing, the adrenalin rush, I think they call it. When it goes away, you shake like this. And, no matter how justified you were, there's a part of your mind that's still reelin' 'cause you killed him. That's a normal reaction. Let me ask you a question."

"Okay."

"Did you intend to kill him?"

"No!"

"Okay. Here's another question. Y'all were wrestlin' over the gun. Could it just as easily have been you who got shot and killed?"

"I guess so." Ruby replied slowly.

The sheriff came around his desk and clasped her hands in his. "Then let's try to focus on the fact that both you and Betty are safe and unharmed. That's what's important. It's never easy to take a life. Be gentle on yourself, and give yourself some time."

"Have you ever killed somebody, Sheriff?" Betty asked.

Jasper sighed heavily. "Once. Few years back a man went crazy off some bad 'shine. Killed his wife and was threatenin' to kill the kids. Took me a while to get past it, but you will." He looked up at a knock on his doorframe. "Yes, Boyd?"

"Sorry to interrupt, Sir, but you asked to be told when Dr. Boone arrived."

"Good. Send him on in." At Ruby's frown, he continued, "Ruby, I asked him here 'cause I figured you could use an old friend right about now. Besides,

I wanted him to take a look at your bumps and bruises and make sure you're all right. Your Pa'd skin me alive if I didn't."

Jake strode into the office, dropping his medical bag on a chair. "Thanks for callin' me, Sheriff Carter. Ruby, you all right?"

Ruby looked up at him, tears in her eyes. "Jake … Jake, I killed him. I …." As she burst into sobs, Jake pulled her up, hugging her as she cried.

The sheriff looked at Betty, gesturing with his head toward the door. "Let's go get you a soda, little lady. We'll come back in a while, after Dr. Boone's had a chance to see to Miz Ruby."

When Ruby's sobs had abated, Jake sat her back down in a chair in front of the sheriff's desk, pulling another chair up next to hers. He held her hands while they talked, gently rubbing his thumbs over the back of her hands. It soothed her, and before long she was able to talk, though tears still occasionally trickled down her cheeks. "It happened so fast. One second he was on top of me, tryin' to yank the gun away, and then … and then it went off and he was dead."

"Ruby, are you hurt?"

She ignored his question. "For years, I was wantin' him dead. I even prayed for it. But now …

314

now, I'd made peace with things. I stopped wantin' him dead, I just wanted him out of my life for good. Now ... now, I feel like it's my fault he's dead."

"That's plain crazy, Ruby. You didn't go lookin' for him, aimin' to hurt him. You didn't cause this. Ray did when he tried to take Betty. I'm just glad you were there to stop him."

"Then why do I feel so guilty? Shouldn't I just be relieved it's over?"

Jake gave a short laugh. "You feel guilty 'cause somebody died at your hand, and that's a real shocker, no matter that he deserved it. You're a good person, not a killer, so of course you're gonna feel guilty. And, I suspect you do feel a sense of relief that he's dead. Just means you're human."

"When'd you get to be so smart, Jake?" Ruby gave him a small smile.

"Well, let's see ... as I recollect, I woke up one morning – it was October 14th, 1930 – and I felt especially smart that mornin'. Just kinda hit me like that."

Ruby laughed. "You are so silly sometimes."

"Yup – Just one of my charms. Now, let me look at that bruise on your cheek. Let's make sure the bone's not broken." Jake gently pushed on her cheek, deciding it was just a bruise. "Anything else? I see some scratches on your arms. From the sidewalk?" At her nod, he pulled a small tube of cream from his bag. "Try a little of this on them to take away the sting. Anything else?"

"Just a sore place in my hip where I landed on the sidewalk. And no, Jake Boone, you'll not be lookin' at that. It'll be fine."

He shrugged and grinned at her. "At least let me know if it gets worse, okay?"

"I can do that. Thanks for being here for me, Jake. It means a lot. You're a good friend."

"I'll always be here for you, Ruby. I'll always be your friend." He shook his head. "My Ma is sore disappointed we're just friends – ruined all her plans." He laughed. "But I finally convinced her we knew what was best for us."

Ruby smiled sadly at him. "I know you had plans for us too. I think maybe I did too, but Jake, after all that happened to me, I just can't …"

"I know, Ruby. I really do understand, and it's okay. God willin' and the creek don't rise, I will have you for a friend all my life. That's sayin' somethin'. And who knows, maybe someday, when we're old and gray we can share a place and bore each other silly with made-up stories about our grand lives."

She laughed. "Now that'd be somethin', wouldn't it?"

Sheriff Carter knocked on the doorframe. "Y'all about done in here? I'm thinkin' we should get you home now. Deputy Boyd and I will take you ladies and your Pa's truck out to the farm."

Ruby stood. "Thanks, Sheriff Carter. Neither of us is fit to be drivin' right now. We'd be grateful for that ride home."

Fifty-Eight

A TIME TO GO HOME

It was the following day, after the sheriff and Deputy Boyd had escorted Ruby and Betty home, before anyone remembered the mail Ruby had picked up at the post office. Sure enough, there was a letter from Celine, asking Ruby to return with Gracie. Ruby read the letter aloud to Betty and Lida, as they sat around the table, shelling peas for supper.

Dearest Ruby,

My friend the lawyer in New Orleans has been most helpful. We are now in possession of all the documents we need to safeguard (I think that is the right word – to keep her safe?) Gracie. My friend has provided us with very legal looking (I do not ask.) papers. There is a letter from Clara to me, giving up rights and custody. There is the judge's order recognizing that, and giving temporary approval of a petition for adoption. The final approval will come in one year. My friend assures me there is no problem.

I hope you do not mind. I know you wanted to be the one to adopt Grace, but my friend thought it would be better if it was me. Because I am a widow and you are a single woman, a court would favor me. It does not matter. We will love and raise this little girl together.

Please come home soon. It is too quiet here without you and Gracie. And Norma says she wants her car back.
Regards to your family and to Betty – Celine

"They did it! Ma – they did it. Celine will be adoptin' Gracie, and we'll be raisin' her together." Ruby was beside herself with joy.

"That's great news, darlin'. I'm right happy for you, 'cept now you're gonna be leavin' again." Lida hugged her daughter. "When you fixin' to leave?"

"I reckon come the end of the week. I'll have to check with Sheriff Carter and make sure I'm free to go first. He said there'd be no charges, but I still should check."

"You didn't sleep much last night, did you? I heard you tossin' and turnin'."

"I keep hearin' the bang and seein' the blood. Every time I'd drift off, I'd wake up again, sweatin' and shakin'."

"That'll pass. May take a bit, but it'll pass."

Betty spoke up. "When you go back – I want to go too."

"What? Why ever would you want to do that? You're safe from your Pa here." Ruby was astounded.

"I know, but … if you can face down your monster like you did, I figure I can face down mine. If you let me, I'll stay at the dairy. I can earn my keep, you know."

"I know that, but … I don't want you to have to face down your Pa like I did Ray. That's gonna haunt me the rest of my life."

"I know."

"What'll you do when your Pa comes out to the dairy again, lookin' for you? He will, you know."

"I'll tell him 'No!', and I'll keep on sayin' it till he finally gets it through his drunk skull I want no part of him. I'm not afraid to stand up to him anymore. Maybe you could teach me how to shoot too, just so I could …"

"No! There'll be no learnin' to shoot in your future! You don't want …" Ruby paused, shaking her head. "Let me think on it a while – if you should come back with me. Let me think on it." She stood up. "I'm gonna go see if Pa needs help finishin' up in the barn. And tell him about Celine's letter."

"You do that. Betty and I can handle Gracie and gettin' supper on the table. Go."

Fifty-Nine

THE REWARD

It was another three days before Ruby felt up to going to town to see the sheriff. The shooting had shaken her badly, and she needed some time to try to recapture the peace she'd felt earlier. She also didn't feel like getting stared at by any of the townsfolk, who by now knew what had happened.

"Mornin', Miss Ruby," Sheriff Carter greeted her. "I was just about to head out to the farm to see you. How you doin'?"

"Fair to middlin'. I guess. Not sleepin' too good, but I guess that's normal."

"Sure is. Give it time. What brings you into town this mornin'?"

"I wanted to ask if I'm free to travel, to go back to North Carolina. You said you didn't think there'd be charges for killin' Ray, but I wanted to make sure."

"I ran it past Judge Wilson yesterday, and he agrees with me. So you can head back whenever you want. Just leave me your address there, in case I need any more details from you."

"Thank you so much!"

"And, I've got some more good news for you. It seems that Ray's been right busy the last couple of years. Looks like he moved over to Richmond and got himself hooked up with a pair of bank robbers. The FBI figures they were responsible for three banks bein' robbed near there. They were tripped up tryin' to rob a US Mail truck about six months ago. Caught his partners, but Ray went on the lam. FBI's been lookin' for him ever since."

"Can't say I'm surprised, really." Ruby shook her head in disgust.

"Best part is, there's a reward. You got some money comin' to you – a thousand dollars!"

"Even though he's dead? They don't care?"

"Even though he's dead." Jasper grabbed his hat off the hook in his office. "I'm thinkin' that money might come in real handy, help you make a go of that dairy farm. Why don't we head on down to the bank, and I'll see that you get it now, so you don't have to wait?"

"I'd be much obliged. We can really use that money." Ruby gave a short laugh. "Can't believe he was worth that much money to the government, but I'm glad. Before we go, there's somethin' else I wanted to ask you about." Ruby explained how Betty wanted to go back with her. "I understand her wantin' to face her fears, but I'm worried her Pa will try somethin' she can't handle. Is there a way you could check with the sheriff in Hickory and see if he thinks it's safe for her to come back with me?"

"Why sure. Come on back into my office and I'll give him a call. Not sure he'll know, but we can try." Within a few minutes, the operator had the sheriff in Hickory on the line and Jasper explained why he was calling. "Uh huh … uh huh …right. You don't say? For how long?" Jasper shook his head. "Well, thank you kindly, Sheriff. You've been a big help." After he hung up the phone, he looked at Ruby and laughed. "I'd say it's safe for the girl to go home with you. Her Pa nigh unto killed a man in a bar fight. He's gonna be in jail for a long, long time, somethin' like twenty years accordin' to the sheriff." He stood. "Now, let's go get you that money."

Sixty

YOU NEVER KNOW

April 1939

Only about another hour to go, Ruby thought to herself. It had been a fairly easy drive. They left the farm in Virginia just after noon, making several stops along the way for gas or food, much like their trip three months before. But this time, the mood in the car was very different. They felt, if not exactly carefree, then peaceful, relieved. Not only were the plans to adopt Gracie going through, but Ray was dead, and Betty's Pa was in jail.

Ruby was looking forward to getting back to the dairy. In the few months they'd been gone. Gracie, now almost nine months old, had begun to crawl and pull herself up on things. Ruby smiled, knowing there'd be a lot of cooing and hugging going on when the others saw how much the baby had grown.

It had been hard saying good-bye to her parents again, but when she left, Ruby made them promise to once again come celebrate Thanksgiving at the dairy. That had become the norm; Lida and Tom would head to Hickory for Thanksgiving, and Ruby would come visit them in Roanoke sometime each spring. Some of the reward money had gone to installing a phone at the Malcolm's farm, and that would also help them keep in touch.

The large basket in the car's trunk was full of welcome treats her Ma and Pa had packed up for them. There were some of Lida's canned green beans, hams and bacon, and nestled in the bottom of the basket were a couple of jars of rhubarb jam. Those were Lida's latest entry into the ongoing rhubarb jam contest between her and Della. Ruby chuckled, anticipating Della's reaction.

It was almost full dark now, and Ruby glanced over at Betty. The girl had fallen asleep, leaning against the side window, Gracie snuggled up next to her. Ruby started softly humming the song she'd heard playing on the radio at the small café where they'd stopped for supper, something called 'I've got a Pocketful of Dreams' by Bing Crosby. Ruby smiled, remembering what Jake had said about when they got old and gray, about sharing a place and boring each other with grand stories about their lives. *You never know about the future, Jake, you never know. It just might happen.*

HISTORICAL NOTES

Virginia during the Great Depression:

Virginia felt the impact of the Great Depression less than many states, but it did not escape unscathed. The state's economy was a balance between agriculture, industry, and commerce, and Federal Government expenditures in Washington and Norfolk helped to minimize the effects of the Depression.

In 1932, Virginia's state government cut back on spending in order to balance their budget. Over 60% of the schools reduced their school terms to less than eight months. Schools were closed and teachers' salaries were cut. Norfolk fired teachers and closed kindergartens.

The Moonshine Conspiracy Trial:

The Moonshine Conspiracy Trial of 1935 led to the indictment of 80 people, engaged in the production and distribution of moonshine whiskey in

Franklin County, Virginia. The ring of conspirators was accused of defrauding the government of over 5 million dollars in whiskey excise taxes (around 95 million dollars in today's currency). Local sheriffs and government officials allegedly charged the moonshine distillers for protection from federal law enforcement agencies (aka the revenuers). However, there is some evidence that the governor of Virginia told law enforcement to simply fine the moonshiners whenever they could in order to ease congestion in the state's jails and courts.

The trial took place in Roanoke, Virginia (Which was not in Franklin County), and it lasted around ten weeks. The verdict came down on July 1, 1935, and resulted in over 20 convictions, including several government officials and officers of the law. The Moonshine Conspiracy Trial had little effect on the production of moonshine in Franklin County as the sentences were light, and many of those convicted returned to making illegal whiskey even before they served their jail time.

Salem Veterans Affairs Medical Center:

On October 19, 1934, President Franklin D Roosevelt dedicated the new Salem Veterans Affairs Medical Center in Roanoke, Virginia. It was his first visit to the area, in fact, it was the first official visit of any president to the area. The hospital had 472 operating beds, and included a pharmacy, a lab, a dental office, and an x-ray facility. While it was a state-of-the art facility, there was also a hog and cattle farm on site, and patients at the hospital worked there as part of their therapy.

Snickers Candy Bar

The Snickers candy bar was introduced in 1930 by the American company Mars, Incorporated. It was named after creator Frank Mars' favorite horse. It was then, and still is, a confection made up of nougat, peanuts, caramel, and covered in chocolate.

Greyhound Bus Lines

The Greyhound Bus Lines was started in Hibbing, MI in 1914. Originally called the Hupmobile (The founder was a salesman for Hupp Motors.), it transported workers between towns. In 1929, the buses were painted gray so as not to show as much road dirt, and the company was renamed Greyhound. In 1930, a silver greyhound was added as the company mascot, and radio ads gave the company nationwide success. The buses were air conditioned in 1938, long before cars.

ABOUT THE AUTHOR

Karen D. McIntyre lives in La Plata, Maryland, with her husband, Lew, and three cats, Bogie, Phil, and Davy. She retired after twenty-eight years teaching Language Arts and Social Studies in middle and high schools. Karen is a voracious reader of multiple genres. While she is a gym rat, she is also adept at wine tasting, and loves to travel.

Made in the USA
Monee, IL
16 June 2020